The Cats of Tanglewood Forest

The Cats of Tanglewood Forest

WRITTEN BY ILLUSTRATED BY

CHARLES DE LINT   CHARLES VESS

LB

LITTLE, BROWN AND COMPANY

New York   Boston

Text copyright © 2013 by Charles de Lint
Illustrations copyright © 2013 by Charles Vess

Little, Brown and Company

Hachette Book Group
237 Park Avenue, New York, NY 10017
Visit our website at www.lb-kids.com

Little, Brown and Company is a division of Hachette Book Group, Inc.
The Little, Brown name and logo are trademarks of Hachette Book Group, Inc.

The publisher is not responsible for websites (or their content) that are not owned
by the publisher.

First Edition: March 2013
Based on the book *A Circle of Cats*, written by Charles de Lint and illustrated by Charles Vess,
originally published in 2003 by Viking.

Library of Congress Cataloging-in-Publication Data
De Lint, Charles, 1951–
The cats of Tanglewood Forest / written by Charles de Lint ; illustrated by Charles Vess. — 1st ed.
p. cm.
Summary: Twelve-year-old Lillian, an orphan who loves roaming the woods looking for fairies when her chores are done, is bitten by a deadly snake and saved through the magical forest creatures in this expansion on the author's and illustrator's previous work, A circle of cats.
ISBN 978-0-316-05357-0
[1. Magic—Fiction. 2. Cats—Fiction. 3. Trees—Fiction. 4. Snakebites—Fiction.
5. Orphans—Fiction.] I. Vess, Charles, ill. II. De Lint, Charles, 1951– Circle of cats. III. Title.
PZ7.D383857Tan 2013
[Fic]—dc23
2011042982

10 9 8 7 6 5 4 3 2

WOR

Printed in the United States of America

Book design by Saho Fujii

For my two best gals:
MaryAnn and Clare

—Charles de Lint

For Miso (I miss you, buddy) and June,
who peeked through the trees and saw
the very first circle of cats

—Charles Vess

And for Joe Monti,
who thought a longer story was a good idea

Contents

The Cats of Tanglewood Forest

CHAPTER ONE

The Awful, Dreadful Snake

Once there was a forest of hickory and beech, sprucy-pine, birch and oak. It was called the Tanglewood Forest. Starting at the edge of a farmer's pasture, it seemed to go on forever, uphill and down. There were a few abandoned homesteads to be found in its reaches, overgrown and uninhabitable now, and deep in a hidden clearing there was a beech tree so old that only the hills themselves remembered the days when it was a sapling.

Above that grandfather tree, the forest marched up to the hilltops in ever-denser thickets of rhododendrons and brush until nothing stood between the trees and stars. Below it, a creek ran along the bottom of a dark narrow valley, no more than a trickle in some places, wider in others. Occasionally the water tumbled down rough staircases of stone and rounded rocks.

On a quiet day, when the wind was still, the creek could be heard all the way up to where the old beech stood. Under its branches cats would come to dream and be dreamed. Black cats and calicos, white cats and marmalade ones, too. Sometimes they exchanged gossip or told stories about L'il Pater, the trickster cat. More often they lay in a drowsy circle around the fat trunk of the ancient beech that spread its boughs above them. Then one of them might tell a story of the old and powerful Father of Cats, and though the sun might still be high and the day warm, they would shiver and groom themselves with nervous tongues.

But they hadn't yet gathered the day the orphan girl fell asleep among the beech's roots, nestling in the weeds and long grass like the gangly, tousle-haired girl she was.

Her name was Lillian Kindred.

She hadn't meant to fall asleep, but she was a bit like a cat herself, forever wandering in the woods, chasing after squirrels and rabbits as fast as her skinny legs could take her when the fancy struck, climbing trees like a possum, able to doze in the sun at a moment's notice. And sometimes with no notice at all.

This morning she'd been hunting fairies down by the creek, where it pooled wide for a spell. The only way you could cross it here was by the stepping-stones laid out in an irregular pattern from one bank to the other.

"Fairies won't go across the water," the midwife Harlene Welch told her, "but they do like to gather on the stones. Creep up on them all quiet-like and you can catch them sunning there like dragonflies."

The trouble was, dragonflies were all she ever found by the creek. She never found fairies anywhere, no matter how hard she looked, though some days she could feel them in the air around her, tiny invisible presences as quick as honeybees. The air would hum with the rapid beat of their wings, but no matter how quickly she turned and spun, they were never there when she looked.

She and Aunt lived miles from anyone, deep in the hills, halfway down the slope between their apple orchard and the creek. It seemed the perfect place to find fairies if ever there was one, and if the stories the old folks told were true. But no matter how quietly Lillian prowled through the woods, no matter how often she crept up on a mushroom fairy ring, the little people were never there.

~

"Don't you go troubling the spirits," Aunt told her on more than one occasion. "They were here before us, and they'll still be here when we're gone. Best you just leave them be."

"But why?"

"Because they're not partial to being bothered by some little red-haired girl who's got nothing better to do than stick her nose in other folks' business. When it comes to spirits, it's best not to draw their attention. Elsewise you never know what you might be calling down on yourself."

That was hard advice for a young girl.

"I'm not troubling anyone," she would tell the oldest apple tree in the orchard as she lay on the ground, looking up into its leaves. "I just want to say hello hello."

But it was hard to say hello to fairies she couldn't find.

~

One afternoon Lillian and Aunt were working in the corn patch. Aunt pulled the weeds up with her

hoe while Lillian followed behind and put them in a basket. Aunt was humming some old tune, the way she always did. "Get Up John," maybe. Or that old, sad song "The Little Girl and the Dreadful Snake."

"I wouldn't hurt the fairies," Lillian said. "I just want a look at them is all. Where's the harm in that?"

Aunt broke off her humming and leaned on her hoe.

"Maybe there is and maybe there isn't," she said. "I reckon only those little spirits could tell you the one way or t'other. I just know what my pappy told me. He said, 'You be careful 'round the spirits. Once they take an interest in you . . . well, sometimes they take a liking, and sometimes they don't. They're like the wild cats thataway.'"

"I like the cats."

Aunt nodded. "And I reckon they like you, seeing's how you're giving them a saucer of Annabelle's milk every morning the way you do. I don't mind 'em coming 'round. They keep the mice away. But you got to remember with a wild cat, you could be a-petting him calm as you please one day, and the next it's a-scratching and a-clawing at you for no good reason you could ever put a finger on. There's no accounting for them. No, sir. *That's* what the spirits are like, girl. Folks like you and me, we can't predict what they'll do."

"Maybe the fairies would like me the way the cats do."

Aunt smiled and went back to her hoeing.

"I've heard tell," she said as she worked the dirt, "that they're kin of a kind. The way a squirrel and a rat are kin, them both being rodents. Pappy said everything living in the deep woods has got a bit of magic in it, but cats have more'n most. You ask the preacher and he'll tell you it's because they all got a bit of the devil in 'em."

Lillian shook dirt from the weeds and dropped them in her basket. She liked it when Aunt talked about fairies and such. Most times she only told Lillian about practical things to do with running the farm.

"Have you ever seen a spirit?" she asked Aunt.

That earned her another smile. "Live in these hills long enough and sooner or later you'll have seen pretty much everything. Your Uncle Ulyss used to tease me something fierce, but I hold to this day that one time I saw L'il Pater crossing the bottom of the field. He was walking on his hind legs, just like a little man, with a floppy hat on his head, big black boots on his feet, and a bag hanging on a stick he had slung over his shoulder. And following on behind him was a line of cats of every size and color."

"What did you *do*?"

"I didn't do anything. I just stood there with my eyes big as saucers, staring and staring until the woods swallowed 'em all up like they'd never been there." She laughed. "Which is what Ulyss said was the case. But I'll tell you, I didn't see a cat around this farm for two weeks after. And when they come back, they were slinking around like they'd spent the time they were gone doing nothing but drinking moonshine and dancing, and every time they had to move, it made them ache something fierce."

Aunt went back to humming and Lillian tried to imagine what she would have done if she'd been the one to see L'il Pater.

$\sim$

The next morning she did her chores, just like every morning. She fed the chickens, throwing an extra handful of grain into the grass for the sparrows and other small birds that waited for the promise of her bounty in the branches of the wild rosebushes that grew nearby. She milked Annabelle, their one cow, and set out a saucer for the stray cats that would come out of the forest while she put the cow out to pasture and brought the milk in to Aunt. After a breakfast of biscuits and honeyed tea, she weeded the vegetable patch. If Aunt didn't have any other chores for her, and she was done with her lessons, the rest of the day was hers to do what she wanted.

She set off on a ramble, running up the hill to leave a piece of one of her breakfast biscuits under the boughs of the Apple Tree Man.

That's what Aunt called the oldest apple tree in their orchard gone wild. He stood near the very top of the hill, overlooking the meadow dotted with wild-flowers and beehives and the other apple trees.

"Why do you call him that?" Lillian had asked the first time she'd heard his name. "Is there a real man living in the tree?"

He'd be a gnarled, twisty sort of a man, she thought, to live in that old, twisty tree. She probably daydreamed as much about him as she did fairies, especially when she was lying under his branches. Sometimes when she dozed there she imagined she could hear a distant voice telling stories that she never remembered when she woke.

"I don't know the why or where of it," Aunt replied. "But that's what we've always called the oldest apple tree. Only we didn't leave food out for him, like you do." She shook her head. "You're just feeding the raccoons and squirrels."

Lillian didn't think so—not at all. There was an Apple Tree Man, just like there were fairies and magic cats. He was shy, that was all. Private. But one day all the spirits of the Tanglewood Forest would know that she meant them no harm, and they would come to her and they'd all be friends.

~

So, with her chores done, breakfast finished, and the Apple Tree Man fed, she went down into the hollow. She wandered upstream from the stepping-stones to where the creek tumbled down a staircase of rocks, enjoying the change of temperature on her arms when she walked from sunlight into shadow and then out again. By the waterfall she balanced on the slick rocks and lichen, poking at the shiny pebbles under- water with a stick until she felt the weight of some- one's attention upon her.

Looking up, she found herself face-to-face with a

handsome, white-tailed deer. He stood on the edge of a tangle of rhododendrons, with the sprucy-pine and yellow birch rising up the hillside behind him.

Deer were almost as good as fairies, so far as Lillian was concerned.

"Hello hello, you," she said.

When he turned and bolted, she ran in pursuit. Not to catch him, not to scare him. Just for the fun of seeing how fast they both could run.

They ran uphill and down. They ran through thickets of hickory and yellow birch, across sudden

meadows where the grass and weeds slapped against their legs, up rock-strewn slopes, dusky with moss and ferns, and back down into the hollow, where the creek ran with them. They ran and ran, the deer bounding gracefully, Lillian scrambling and leaping, but no less quick for that.

Sometimes she could almost touch him. Sometimes

all she could see of him was the flash of a white tail, but when he saw that she was falling behind, he would pretend to catch his own breath, only to bolt away again as she drew near.

They ran through familiar fields and meadows and deep into parts of the forest where Lillian had never been before. The trees were older here, and the thickets sometimes so dense that she had to wriggle under the ones that the deer bounded over so gracefully.

That was how she finally found
herself lying under that grandfather beech tree in its hidden clear-
ing, the deer gone his own way while she collapsed in a
tangle of limbs in the tall grass and fell asleep.

And that was where the snake bit her.

~

It was an awful, dreadful snake, like in that old song
Aunt sometimes sang. Lillian never even knew it was
there under the tree with her until it struck.

The snake had been sleeping when Lillian curled
up in the grass, all coiled up only inches from her
foot. Dreaming, Lillian moved a leg suddenly, kicking at a milkweed head in her dream, which, in turn,

disturbed the snake's own drowsy nap. The bright pain from its first strike woke her, but by then it was already too late. It struck a second time, a third. She tried to rise, to call Aunt for help, but the venom stole her strength and dropped her back onto the ground, shivering and cold.

She knew she was dying, just like the little girl in the song.

The fog of pain already lay too thick for her to see the cats come out of the long grass. Some of them she would have known because they came to visit her in the morning. Others were strangers, cats no one saw, they lived so deep in the forest, but they, too, knew of the skinny, half-wild girl who fed their cousins.

The one Lillian called Big Orange—almost the size of a bobcat, with the russet fur of a fox—was in the lead. He pounced on the snake and bit off its head, *snap*, just like that. Black Nessie batted the head away with a quick swipe of her paw. Two of the kittens jumped on the snake's thrashing body, growling and clawing and biting, but it was already in its death throes and couldn't harm anyone else. The other cats gathered in their circle, only this time, instead of calling up cat dreams, they had a dying girl in the middle of them.

Lillian wasn't aware of any of this. She was falling up into a bright tunnel of light, which was an odd experience, because she'd never fallen up before. She hadn't even known it was possible.

She wasn't scared now, or even in pain. She just wished the voices she heard would stop talking, because they were holding her back. They wouldn't let her fall all the way up into the tunnel of light.

"We have to save her."

"We can't. It's too late."

"Unless . . ."

"Unless we change her into something that isn't dying."

"But Father said we must never again—"

"I'll accept the weight of Father's anger."

"We all will."

"We'll make her one of our own—then he won't mind."

"He minded that time we gave the mice wings."

"This is different."

"This time we're saving a friend."

They turned their attention to Lillian and woke cat magic under the boughs of their old beech tree. First they swayed back and forth, in time with each other. Then their voices lifted in a strange, scratchy

harmony like a kitchen full of fiddles not quite in tune with each other, but not so out of tune as to be entirely unpleasant. A golden light rose up from their music to glow in the air around them. It hung there, pulsing to the rhythm of their song for a long moment, before it went from cat to cat in the circle, 'round and 'round.

Three times the light went around the circuit before it left them and came to rest on the dying girl in the middle of their circle. The cats lifted their heads. They could see the soul of the girl floating up through the boughs of the beech. Their scratchy song rose higher and the light rose with it, chasing after the soul like a rope of golden light. When it finally caught up, the rope of light wrapped around her, pulling Lillian's soul back into her body.

The cats fell silent, staring at the rise and fall of Lillian's chest, and exchanged pleased looks with one another. But then, frightened by what they had done, by what Father might do when he found out, they re-treated back into the forest.

CHAPTER TWO

The Girl Who Woke Up as a Cat

Lillian woke up and had a long, lazy stretch. What an odd dream, she thought. She lifted a paw, licked it, and had just started to clean her face when she realized what she was doing. She held the paw in front of her face. It was definitely a paw, covered in fur and minus a thumb. Where was her hand?

She looked at the rest of herself and saw only a cat's calico body, as lean and lanky as her own, but covered in fur and certainly not the one she knew.

"What's become of me?" she said.

"You're a kitten," a voice said from above.

She looked up to find a squirrel looking down at her from a branch of the beech. He seemed to be laughing at her.

"I'm not a cat, I'm a girl," she told him.

"And I'm an old hound dog," the squirrel replied.

Then he made a passable imitation of a hound's mournful howl and bounded off, higher up into the tree.

"But I *am* a girl," Lillian said.

She started to get up but she seemed to have too many legs and sprawled back onto the grass.

"Or at least I was."

She tried to get up again, moving gingerly until she realized that this cat's body she was in knew how to get around. Instead of worrying about how to get up and move, she had to let herself move naturally, the way she did when she was a girl.

This time when she stood she saw the body of the headless snake, and it all came back to her. She backed away, the hair rising all along her spine, her tail puffing out. It hadn't been a dream.

She'd been snakebit. She'd been dying. And then . . . and then . . . what? She remembered a tunnel of light and voices.

Fairies, she thought. The fairies had come to rescue her.

"Squirrel!" she called up into the branches of the tree. "Did you see the fairies? Did you see them change me?"

There was no reply.

"I don't think I want to be a cat," she said.

Now she *really* had to find the fairies.

~

By the time she'd bounded all the way down to the creek, she was more comfortable in her new body, though no happier about being in it. There were no fairies about, but then there never were when she was looking for them. What was she going to do? She couldn't go through the rest of her life as a cat.

Finding a quiet pool along the bank, she looked in. And here was the strangest thing of all: There was her own girl's face looking back at her from the water. When she lifted what was plainly a paw, the reflection lifted a hand.

Lillian sat back on her haunches to consider this.

"They changed you," a voice said from above. "Now you're not quite girl, not quite cat."

She looked up to see an old crow perched on a branch.

"Do you mean the fairies?" she asked.

"No, the cats."

"The cats?" she said. "But why?"

"You were dying. They had no madstone to draw the poison out, nor milk to soak it in, nor hands to

do the work and hold the stone in place. So they did
what they could. They changed you into something
that's not dying."

Lillian had seen a madstone before. Harlene
Welch had one. Her husband found it in the stomach of a deer he was field-dressing, a smooth, flat,
grayish-looking stone about the size of a silver dollar.
You had to soak it in milk and then lay it against the
bite, where it would cling, only falling off when all
the poison had been drawn out. It worked on bites
from both snakes and rabid animals.

"Will I be like this forever?" Lillian asked.

"Maybe, maybe not," the crow said.

"What does that mean?"

"You know the stories," he said. "What was changed
once can be changed again."

"I don't know that story," Lillian said. "I don't
know any stories about snakes. I only know that song
about the awful, dreadful snake, and the little girl
dies in it."

The crow nodded his head. "That's a sad song."

"Can you tell me what to do?"

"Can't."

"But—"

"Not won't," the crow said, "but can't. I know the stories, but the stories don't tell how one thing is changed into another, just that it is. You have to ask someone who knows something about magic."

"Like the cats."

"Well, now," the crow said, "any other day and I'd say yes to that. But that's a big magic those cats did, and they'll be hiding now."

"Hiding from what?"

"You know."

Lillian shook her head. "But I don't. I don't seem to know *anything* anymore."

The crow looked one way, then another.

"Him," he said in a soft croak. "They'll be hiding from him. Cats are magic, but they're not supposed to work magic. He doesn't like that."

Lillian gave a nervous look around herself as well, though she had no idea what she was looking for.

"Who are you talking about?" she whispered.

"The Father of Cats."

Lillian's eyes went wide. "There really *is* a Father of Cats?"

"Says the girl who's always out looking for fairies."

"How do you know that?"

The crow's chest feathers puffed a little.

"Well, now," he said. "There's not much goes on in these woods that I don't know about."

"But you can't help me."

"I didn't say that. The problem is that the Father of Cats is too big a piece of magic for the likes of you or me."

The Father of Cats. Every time the crow said that name, Lillian felt a shiver go running up her spine. There wasn't anybody 'round here didn't know some story about that old black panther who was supposed to haunt these hills. They said he snatched babies right out of their cribs and crunched on their bones up in the boughs of some tall, tall tree. He plucked livestock from the barn and travelers from the road.

When he was angry, thunderstorms rumbled high in the mountains and great winds ripped at the homesteads, rattling shutters and carrying away roofs and sheds.

He was a big dark shadow in the woods, and the only way you knew he was close was by the *pat-pat-pat* of his tail on the ground, and then it was too late. If a black cat was bad luck, the Father of Cats was worse luck still. Some said he was the devil himself, but that was disputed by as many as those who claimed it to be true. Still, most would at least agree that he was a fearsome creature. Maybe not supernatural, but still very, very dangerous.

The worst story Lillian knew about the Father of Cats came from one of the Creek boys—John, or maybe it was Robert. The Creeks lived up on the Kickaha rez, but the boys came by Aunt's from time to time to help with the heavier chores like plowing the corn patch and turning the garden, or fetching and chopping wood. One of those Creeks told her that the Father of Cats could prowl through your dreams. If you caught sight of him there, he'd chase you down until his big jaws chomped down on your head, and then you died. Not just in the dream, but for real.

"Is—is he everything the stories say he is?" Lillian asked the crow now.

The crow nodded. "Depends on the stories you've heard, but probably."

The shiver went up Lillian's spine again.

"Oh, no question," the crow went on, "he's desperately powerful, that bogey panther. Folks like us, we don't want to get on his bad side. We don't even want him turning his attention our way. So you can't blame those cats for hiding."

"But what do I do?"

"You need to find you a body that's got enough magic in her she won't be scared, but she's also got to be somewise less formidable than him, so that he doesn't see her as a threat. Someone like Old Mother Possum."

"I've never heard of her."

"That's because she lives in your new world, not the one you came from."

"I don't want to be in a new world," Lillian said.

"Maybe so," the crow said, "but you don't want to go back to the old one just yet, because over there you're a dead little snakebit girl."

"I don't want to be that, either."

"Of course you don't."

"Where do I find her?" Lillian asked.

"You know where the creek splits by the big rocks?"

Lillian nodded.

"Well, just follow that split down into Black Pine Hollow—all the way to where the land goes marshy. Old Mother Possum's got herself a den down there, under a big dead pine. You can't miss that tree."

"Is—is she nice?" Lillian wanted to know.

The crow laughed. "She's a possum that's part witch—what do you think?"

Lillian didn't know what to think, except she wished that mean snake hadn't bitten her in the first place.

"Now, when you go see her," the crow said, "make sure you show the proper respect."

Lillian's fur puffed a little. "I may look like a cat, but I know how to be polite."

"Being polite goes without saying. I meant you should bring her a little something as a token of respect."

"What kind of something?"

"Oh, I don't know. It doesn't have to be big. A

mouse, or a vole. Something tasty, with crunchy bones."

Lillian thought of the squirrel she'd met, and now this crow.

"Do they talk?" she asked.

"Does who talk?"

"The mice and voles."

The crow laughed. "Of course they talk. Everything talks. Just everybody doesn't take the time to listen."

"I couldn't kill a talking mouse."

The crow looked at her in astonishment. "Then how will you eat?"

"I don't know. Do trees and plants talk, too?"

"Pretty much, though it's not so easy to understand them unless they have a spirit living inside to do the translating. Otherwise their conversations are too slow for us to follow." He chuckled. "But if you think a tree is slow, you should try talking to a stone. They can take a year just to tell you their names."

"What's your name?" Lillian asked the crow.

"Well, now," he replied, "there's some that call me Jack, and I'll answer to that."

"Jack Crow," Lillian repeated. "I'm—"

"Lillian. I know."

"Because you know everything that happens in these hills."

The crow preened a feather. "That I do. Now a word of warning, little cat girl," he added. "I know you like those hound dogs at the Welches' farm, but you need to steer clear of them so long as you're walking around in the skin of a cat. You see a dog sniffing around, you just go up a tree and stay there until it's gone. Hounds and foxes and coyotes . . . none of them's your friend—not any longer. There's more than one critter living in these woods that would enjoy the morsel a little cat girl might provide."

"I'm not scared," Lillian said.

"I can see that. But you should be. You're in a dangerous world now."

Lillian thought her own world hadn't been so safe if you could die from a snakebite when all you were doing was minding your own business.

She had a hundred more questions for the crow, but just then the belling sound of Aunt's big iron triangle came ringing down from the farmhouse. Suppertime. The crow flew off and Lillian jumped from stone to stone across the creek and ran up the hill.

She was hungry, but that wasn't why she hurried home. She realized that Aunt would help her, because Aunt always knew what to do. She'd know some cure, or Harlene Welch would. And if neither of them did, one of them would know some old witchy woman with a bottle tree outside her house and magic in her fingers. Aunt might not put much store in spending time looking for fairies, but like most folks in these hills, she was a firm believer in cures and potions, and she knew where to get them.

CHAPTER THREE

Annabelle

ow, what have we here?" Aunt said as Lillian came running up to her.

"It's me, it's me!" she cried. "Lillian."

But unlike the squirrel and the crow, Aunt didn't hear words, only a plaintive mewling. She smiled and picked Lillian up, scratching her under her chin. Lillian couldn't help herself—she immediately started to purr.

"Where did you come from?" Aunt said. She looked off across the fields. "And where *is* that girl?"

"I'm here, I'm here," Lillian cried from her arms.

But Aunt still couldn't understand her. She carried her inside and gave her a saucer of milk, which Lillian immediately began to lap up because, as much as she didn't want to be a cat, it was suppertime and she was hungry from the long day's activities.

When she was done, she wove in and out between Aunt's legs, but while Aunt would bend down to pat her, she was plainly worried and stood at the doorway looking out at where the dusk was drawing long shadows across the hillside.

They had no phone. They had no close neighbors.
So eventually Aunt took the lantern and went out
looking for her niece.

She made her way down to the creek first, Lillian
trailing after her, still a kitten rather than a girl.
Aunt walked almost a mile up the hollow, her lantern
light bobbing in the dark woods, then crossed over
the creek and came back the other way. Lillian followed behind, no longer trying to tell Aunt she was
right here. If Aunt wasn't going to listen to her, there
was nothing she could do.

When they got back to the farm and Aunt went into the house, Lillian made her way to the barn. There were always cats there—maybe one of them was still hiding in some dark corner. She squeezed inside through a crack where the side door hung a bit loose. Something big stirred in the corner. Then Annabelle, Aunt's milk cow, lifted her head. She blinked a couple of times before her gaze settled on Lillian.

"Hmm," she said.

"Hello?" Lillian tried, not sure if the *hmm* was friendly or not.

"I haven't seen a cat in here all day," Annabelle said, "which is unusual enough on its own, but now when one of you finally does come in, there's something not quite right about you."

"That's because I'm a girl, not a cat."

"I see. That is, I don't *see* the girl you say you are, but it does explain why I sense something strange about you. Have we met before? Because there's also something familiar about you."

"I'm Lillian."

"Ah, yes, of course. It's too bad you've changed. I always thought you had a firm but gentle grip."

"I don't have a grip at all now. I don't even have hands."

"I can see that, too. Mind you keep those claws away from my udder."

"I will," Lillian assured her. "I only came in to see if any of the cats were here. But you say they're all gone?"

"Who knows what they're up to?" Annabelle said. "You know cats. They're a flighty bunch, going whichever way the wind blows. No offense."

She shifted her bulk and Lillian felt the movement through the floorboards under her paws. She'd never realized just how *huge* Annabelle was.

"What do you want with the cats?" the cow asked.

"They're the ones who changed me into a kitten."

"Hmm. The old man won't like that."

"Old man?" Lillian asked. "Do you mean the Father of Cats?"

Annabelle nodded. "Though I wouldn't be throwing his name around willy-nilly—not unless you want to call him to you."

"I don't. Jack Crow said he's just like in the stories."

"He is and he isn't. Depends on what stories you've been listening to. But there's no doubt he's a caution."

That was the sort of thing Aunt would say when she meant something was a little bit dangerous, so you should be careful.

"So you've been talking to Jack Crow?" Annabelle asked.

Lillian nodded and told her story.

"Hmm," Annabelle said when Lillian was finished. "I like Jack Crow—he's always full of gossip—but he's a tricksy sort of a fellow. You'd do well to look closely at anything he tells you, just to make sure his advice serves you and not somebody else."

"You mean he was lying to me?"

"Can't say. Old Mother Possum might be able to help you, but she's a bit of a caution herself."

"Jack Crow says she's part witch."

"She is that, and maybe something older, too. But I suppose it can't hurt to talk to her—just saying you find her in a good mood."

That sounded less promising than Lillian would have liked.

"What do you think I should do?" she asked.

"Hmm."

"If you don't mind telling me, that is."

"I think you should be comfortable with who you are," Annabelle finally said.

"But I'm a girl."

"You *were* a girl. Now you're a cat."

"But—"

"The trouble with magic," Annabelle said, "is that it never really lets go. If you work one magic to undo another, you might end up with a bigger problem than you had in the first place."

"You mean, if I'm turned back into a girl, I'll be dying again. Or already dead."

"That, too. But I was thinking more of how everything we do wheels and spins through the world around us, leaving its mark on everything else."

"I don't understand."

"Hmm."

"I'm sorry."

"Don't be," Annabelle said. "It just means I wasn't being clear. Let me put it another way. Maybe there's a reason why the snake bit you, the cats changed you, and you're no longer a girl. Maybe there's something you can learn from being a cat instead of a little girl."

"What kind of something?"

Annabelle gave a slow shake of her head. "It's not my journey, so how could I even begin to guess?"

Finding answers was as elusive as finding fairies, Lillian thought.

"I'm sorry I can't be of more help," Annabelle said. "I always liked the little girl you were. Maybe you should go find Old Mother Possum. Maybe she can see a better way for you than I can."

"I suppose," Lillian said.

Annabelle gave another *hmm*—a long, slow one—and Lillian realized the cow had fallen asleep once more.

She thought of Jack Crow's directions.

Just follow that split down into Black Pine Hollow—all the way to where the land goes marshy. Old Mother Possum's got herself a den down there, under a big dead pine.

She supposed that was what she had to do: be brave and just go.

When she left the barn, she saw the bob of Aunt's lantern, still searching through the meadow and the forest nearby. In a little while she'd probably go down the path to the Welches' farm, and then they'd all be out looking for her. She wished she could assure Aunt that she was all right, but Lillian only had a cat's voice, and Aunt didn't know how to hear it. She could talk all she wanted, but Aunt would only hear the words as meows.

She turned to look the way she would have to go. The woods seemed very dark, and Jack Crow's warning about dogs and foxes and coyotes rang in her ears. But there was no point in putting it off.

CHAPTER FOUR

Treed by
a Fox

Lillian had never been in the forest at
night before today, but it wasn't as bad as she thought
it would be. In fact, she decided as she walked
through the tall grass behind the barn, it was rather
nice. Magical, almost, from the fireflies dancing in
the meadow below the orchard to the stars twinkling
above. An owl's cry from deeper in the woods sounded
mysterious rather than spooky.

Lillian's cat eyes had such good night vision that it
was easy to see where she was going, and though the

night was filled with strange, scurrying sounds, her nose quickly identified each of them as harmless.

There, a row of small brown birds inside the shelter of a cedar, shifting in restless sleep.

There, a deer stepping delicately through the ferns—a doe, not the young stag she'd chased earlier today.

"Hello hello," Lillian called out to the deer, but the doe was skittish and disappeared among the trees.

Reassured that things weren't nearly as dangerous as her imagination could make them seem, Lillian walked in between the trees with a spring in her step and her tail held high. Her cat body gave her a grace and agility that she'd never before experienced. She bounded with ease over fallen branches and landed lightly on her paws.

The woods thrummed with the activity of nocturnal creatures. The scurrying of voles and mice tempted her to forget about Old Mother Possum and spend the night hunting and pouncing instead. But she remembered her goal and kept moving.

Lillian was deep into the forest when she felt the first pinprick of fear crawl up her spine. She thought she heard something following her. Every time she

stopped to listen—ears flat, body low to the ground—
the echoing footfall she thought she'd heard wasn't
there, so onward she'd go. But the spring in her step
was gone and the dark woods no longer felt like familiar territory or a safe place for a kitten to go jour-
neying.

Jack Crow's warnings returned to her. Why would
she ever think that the forest at night would be safe?
She should have waited until morning to set out.

At that moment, the wind changed direction. It
came from behind her now, bringing the scent of—

She went up the nearest tree, her sharp nails pro-
pelling her along the rough bark to a branch six feet
above the forest floor. Heart drumming in her little
chest, she looked down at the fox that came saunter-
ing out of the shadows—russet fur, black-tipped ears,
and the plume of a tail with a white end that seemed
to glow in the starlight. The fox sat on his haunches
and looked up at her.

"Lordy, lordy," he said. "I have never seen a kitten
go up a tree that fast. Are you running on moonshine or what?"

Lillian could only look down from the safety of her
branch and try to still the rapid beat of her heart.

"What's the matter?" the fox asked when she didn't answer. "Got your own tongue?"

He chuckled at his joke, but his gaze never left her. Lillian dug her claws deeper into the branch.

"Come on now, kitty," he went on. "Why are you hiding up there?"

"I—I'm not a cat," Lillian finally managed. "I'm a girl."

"Sure you are."

"It's true."

"Well, a girl wouldn't be afraid of a little fox, would she? What do you think I'm going to do? Eat you?"

Lillian nodded.

"Well, Girl-in-a-Tree, I've got a belly full of field mice, so I'm not particularly inclined toward eating anything else just about now. But I do need to ask: What makes you think you're safe up there, just saying I *was* inclined to have a little kitty snack?"

"F-foxes can't climb trees."

The fox grinned. "No, but we can jump."

And just like that he was up in the air, his grinning face inches from hers until he dropped back down to the ground. Lillian scrambled up another couple of branches.

"Now, if I had nasty intentions," the fox said, "I could have snatched you right then and there. But I didn't, did I?"

Lillian gave a slow shake of her head.

"And do you know why?"

She shook her head again.

"I'm not looking for my supper," he said. "But I'd be partial to a little conversation."

"Why?"

He shrugged. "Because I'm bored."

"I can talk from where I am," Lillian said, trying to still the tremor in her voice. "I can hear you just fine, so I think you can hear me, too."

"Can and do, but it's giving me a crick in the neck having to look up at you like this."

Better a crick in his neck, Lillian thought, than me in his stomach.

"What's your name?" she asked.

"T. H. Reynolds."

"I'm Lillian. What does the *T.H.* stand for?"

"Truthful and Handsome. My mama always said that a child grows into his name, and I guess she was right, because just look at me."

Lillian couldn't suppress a giggle.

"What's so funny?"

"Are you sure the *H* doesn't stand for *humble*?" she asked.

He gave a disdainful sniff. "Very funny, but it's not bragging if it's true."

Lillian didn't know how much he could be trusted

to be truthful, but she had to admit he was a handsome fox.

"So where were you heading before you ran up that tree?" T.H. asked.

"Black Pine Hollow."

T.H. cocked his head. "Not that it's any of my business, but there's only one reason anybody goes to Black Pine Hollow."

"To see Old Mother Possum."

"Oh, nobody just goes to *see* Old Mother Possum. They go there to ask her to work spells for them. I don't know what you've heard, but playing around with her kind of mojo can be a perilous thing."

Lillian nodded. "That's what Annabelle said."

"Who's Annabelle?"

"Our cow, at my aunt's farm."

T.H. gave her a wide-eyed look. "Cats have their own *farms* now?"

"I told you, I'm not a cat."

"Yeah, yeah. You're really a girl." He stopped to think about that. "Which, I suppose," he went on, "explains why you're going to Black Pine Hollow. What it doesn't explain is why your friend Annabelle is sending you there on your own."

"She didn't. She was just warning me to be careful—same as you. Jack Crow's the one who told me about her first."

"Jack Crow told you," T.H. repeated.

"He told me to be polite and bring her a present. I'm not so sure it's a good idea to visit a possum witch, but what am I supposed to do? I'm a girl, not a cat, but I can't just be changed back, because then I'll be a dead snakebit girl. I need someone to magic the change so that I'm a girl *and* alive."

T.H. shook his head. "This sure isn't boring, but I have to tell you, I don't know what you're talking about."

So Lillian related the whole story, from when she started chasing the stag to where they were now.

"Now that is a tall, tall tale," T.H. said.

"It's true!"

"I didn't say it wasn't. It's just . . . you hear the stories, but you never expect to rub up against one your ownself."

"It's even less fun being stuck in the middle of one. But now you see why I have to go to Black Pine Hollow."

"I do," T.H. said. "And I'd like to come with you—

oh, don't look at me like that. On my word of honor, I won't try to eat you, or cause you any harm. I'm just curious how this will all turn out."

Lillian sighed. She didn't know what to do. Jack Crow told her not to trust hounds and foxes and coyotes. Annabelle told her not to trust Jack Crow. T.H. was telling her to trust him.

"You promise?" she asked.

Because she realized that if she went through the woods with a fox at her side, no one else was likely to bother her.

"I do, indeed."

Uncertain, Lillian came down the tree, which was harder and less dignified than going up. She had to back down, claws digging deep into the bark. The last few feet she let herself go and landed with a small *thump* on the ground. Once there she held herself still, every nerve tense as she waited for the fox to pounce upon her. But T.H. kept his word.

She turned to look at him. He was *so* much bigger from this new perspective.

"Sometimes," T.H. said, "Mama said the *T* in my name stands for *Trustworthy*, which is a lot like *Truthful*. I'm glad you gave me the chance to prove myself."

"I'm not afraid," Lillian told him.

"You should be not of me," he added at her look of alarm, "but of what that possum witch might do."

"I don't know any stories about possum witches," Lillian said. "I don't know any about possums at all, except for the one about why they have hairless tails."

That one she got from one of the many Creek aunts by way of John Creek. He was always bribing her to help him when he was chopping and stacking wood, and a story was the best bribe—especially if it came from the aunts.

The Creek aunts weren't at all like her aunt. They were tall and a little scary—especially Aunt Nancy, maybe because she was a medicine woman, and everybody knew to be careful around bottle witches and medicine women. The Creek aunts had long memories that held all the tribal memories and herb lore of the Kickaha. Aunt got her own herb lore from them, and Lillian got their stories through John or one of the other Creek boys.

In the old days, this story went, Possum had a glorious tail that he never tired of parading in front of Rabbit. This was just meanness on Possum's part, because until Bear pulled it off in a fight, Rabbit's tail had been just as glorious. But after the fight, all he had left was a fluffy tuft.

Still, with the help of Cricket, who cut the hair from Possum's tail when he was supposed to be grooming it, Rabbit got some retribution. Possum was so embarrassed when the other animals saw him with his hairless tail that he fainted dead away—something possums still do to this day.

Of course it was just a story, but when Lillian thought about all that had happened to her since she'd fallen asleep under the beech tree, she supposed it could be true.

"Do you think it's true?" she asked the fox.

T.H. laughed. "Who knows? But I sure wouldn't go repeating it in front of her."

"She's really so dangerous?"

"Only one way to find out," T.H. told her. "If you're feeling up to it . . ."

"I have to go. It's that, or be a kitten forever."

"It's your choice."

"Jack Crow said I should bring a present—to show my respect."

"You mentioned that," T.H. said. "Did he say what kind of present?"

"He seemed to think a mouse or a vole."

"Wouldn't hurt," T.H. said, "but I don't know as it would help much, either. Might seem like a bribe, and not a very fancy one."

"But I want her to like me."

"No, you don't. Possum witches are a whole different thing from folks like you and me. You might as well try to make friends with a stone or a tree."

"I like stones and trees."

T.H. smiled. "Sure you do. But you can't go running in the fields with them, or play ball, or have any kind of a decent conversation, so what's the point?"

"I don't know. Stones are good to sit on, and I like sleeping under trees—except for when snakes sneak up and bite me."

"I think you're stalling."

"I guess I am," Lillian admitted. "But not any-more."

So off they went, the tall fox with a kitten trotting at his side, down the treed slopes to where the creek split.

CHAPTER FIVE

Old Mother Possum

*L*illian had only ever caught glimpses
of foxes before this—quick flashes of their russet fur
across a meadow, or a half-hidden shape in some
distant trees. She'd never realized how sleek they
were, how delicate and graceful, the economy of their
movement. T.H. moved through the forest like the
melody of a well-known song, in perfect harmony
with his surroundings.

She kept stealing glances at him while she bounded
along, trying to keep up. Handsome was a good name
for him, and Truthful, too, it seemed. When they got

to the creek, he jumped easily from stone to stone to reach the other side. Lillian followed in his wake.

She'd crossed by these stepping-stones a hundred times—but that was always in her human form, with her longer legs. Even with her agile cat body, she slipped on the last rock and would have fallen into the creek if T.H. hadn't snapped her up by the nape of her neck. She shivered for a moment, imagining the worst as she hung dangling from his teeth, but he only set her down on the ground, safe and dry.

"You're a feisty little thing," he said, "no question. But you need to pay more attention to your size. Your legs aren't as long as mine."

"They used to be," she told him. "They were even longer."

He smiled. "That's as may be, but you're stuck at this size now."

"Only until I get some help from Old Mother Possum."

His smile faded.

"We'll see about that," he said, and set off again.

"You don't have to be so grouchy," Lillian said.

But she worried about T.H.'s sudden change of mood. If the possum witch made him this uneasy, how dangerous *was* she? Maybe she should have caught a vole after all.

~

The ground soon grew marshy underfoot. T.H. didn't seem to like having wet feet any more than Lillian did. He took a winding way through the marsh, avoiding the soggy ground wherever he could. Lillian hopped along after him, but the limitations of her smaller shape meant she was soon soaked to her belly.

It seemed to take a long time before they finally saw the tall dead pine rising from a small hillock ahead of them. Lillian hesitated. Lit only by the light of a three-quarter moon that had just topped the rim of the hollow, it seemed an ominous place. She could hear the almost inaudible *clink* of small bottles tapping against one another.

"I didn't know she was a bottle witch," Lillian whispered.

"She's not quite possum, not quite human," T.H. said. "Truth is, I don't know what she is."

You never went to a bottle witch with a trivial concern—that's what Aunt always said. Well, being

changed from a dying girl into a kitten wasn't trivial any way you might stretch it. Still . . .

Lillian swallowed, her mouth dry.

"We've come this far," she said, trying to keep the reluctance from her voice. "No point in stopping here."

T.H. nodded. "Except you go on from here on your own."

"W-what? Why?"

She was going to add, You're not scared, are you? But she didn't suppose he'd appreciate that. Being changed into a kitten was her predicament, not his, and she couldn't very well expect him to put himself in danger for her.

"Old Mother Possum and I—we have some history," T.H. said. "I ate her husband, and I don't think she took too kindly to that."

"You *ate* her husband?"

T.H. shrugged. "He was just lying there in the middle of a game trail one evening. What was I supposed to do?"

"Not eat him?"

"I'm a fox. It's what we do."

"I suppose. But I can see why she'd be mad at you."

"She's not," T.H. said. "I'm still standing here,

aren't I? She doesn't *know* that I ate him. But if I get any closer, I'll bet she'll smell it on me, and then there'll be trouble."

"So I have to go on . . . alone?"

T.H. gave her shoulder a nudge with his muzzle.

"Come on now," he said. "I thought nothing scared you."

"I-I'm not scared. It's just . . . maybe I should wait until morning."

"An old witch like that," T.H. said, "she'll be fast asleep during the day. Probably won't take it well, being woken up and all."

Lillian shuddered, and then she squared her small shoulders. "Wish me luck," she said.

"I do."

"Thanks for coming this far with me—and for catching me back at the creek."

"My pleasure. Like I said, I was bored. Now I'm anything but. I'll wait here for you."

"You will?"

T.H. smiled. "Sure. I want to see where your story goes next."

Lillian was about to tell him that he was nothing like she thought a fox would be, except she realized that she was only stalling again—putting off what she didn't want to do. Aunt used to say, "There's those that talk, and those that do. Which do you think gets the thing done?"

It wasn't a question that Aunt ever expected an answer to.

"I'll see you later," Lillian told T.H.

Without T.H. leading the way, she had a harder time judging where the ground was solid and where it would turn to mush under her paws. By the time she reached the hillock where the big dead pine stood, she was caked with mud and soaked right through. She shook herself, spraying mud and smelly marsh water in all directions, making the bottles on the tree clink and rattle even louder.

There were dozens of the little bottles—dark blue and brown glass, the kind used for medicines and tinctures. They banged and clinked against each other in an eerie chorus while Lillian froze, holding her breath until they stopped moving. But she knew it was too late. The noise would have already warned the possum witch that she was here.

What if the witch wouldn't
listen to her? She was just
a bedraggled kitten. What if the
witch just turned her into something
even less appealing than a cat? A frog, maybe. Or a
mosquito. A clump of weeds.

She looked back the way she'd come. Should she try to escape while she could? There was no sign of T.H. No sound except for the cries of the peepers and the hum of insects. She turned back to the dead pine and her heart caught in her throat.

Old Mother Possum was standing under its bare branches, among the bottles.

Lillian hadn't expected her to fit her name as well as she did—neither a woman nor a possum, she was rather some odd combination of the two. She stood just under three feet—tall for a possum, short for a woman, but much bigger than the kitten Lillian was. Her eyes were so dark they didn't seem to have pupils. There was a long possum shape to her face, and her dark gray hair was pulled back in a wispy bun. Even her skin seemed gray, but that was only because of a thin covering of fine possum fur. She wore a deerskin dress decorated with quills and cowrie shells and intricate beaded patterns. Her thin feet—vaguely human-foot-shaped—were bare but still furry.

"Well, now," she said after studying Lillian for a long moment, "you're not as big as I expected."

"Ex-expected?" Lillian repeated.

How could she have been expected? Lillian thought, but then she remembered that the strange little woman *was* a witch. . . .

"I mean I didn't expect a muddy little kitten. The bottles told me someone was coming, but they seemed to think you were much bigger."

"I'm not really a cat," Lillian said. "I'm a girl."

"Are you sure?"

"Look," Lillian said.

She went over to a small pool of swamp water and lifted a paw to point out her reflection. In the water, a girl crouched, pointing with her hand. Old Mother Possum squinted, studying the reflection for a long moment.

"Now, isn't that interesting," she said.

"It's not so interesting when it's happening to you."

Old Mother Possum shrugged. "Everything is a lesson if you're willing to learn something from it."

This was too much like what Annabelle had been saying, and not what Lillian wanted to hear. She knew all about lessons. Aunt schooled her in reading and writing and arithmetic four afternoons a week, making her study until her head hurt. But she'd trade that in a moment for whatever this supposed lesson was.

"I just want to be a girl again," Lillian said. "Can you help me?"

Old Mother Possum turned her dark gaze in Lillian's direction.

"Please?" Lillian added.

"Why should I help you?"

Lillian knew she should have brought a present, but since she hadn't, she fell back on the reason Aunt would give in a situation like this.

"Because it's the neighborly thing to do?" she said.

"How are we neighbors?" Old Mother Possum asked. "I've never seen you before."

"I live on the farm on the other side of the creek, then up the hill."

"Oh. So you're *that* little girl."

Lillian squirmed, not knowing if the possum witch meant *that* as a good or a bad thing. The old woman stood there scratching her chin, looking from Lillian to the reflection and then back again.

"That's a powerful spell you've got on you," she finally said. "Who's got that kind of mojo in these hills?"

Lillian let out a breath that she hadn't been aware of holding.

"It was the cats," she said, and she related how she'd been snakebit and then changed into a kitten.

Old Mother Possum gave a slow nod. "Oh, he's not going to like that."

Lillian didn't have to ask who she meant—not anymore. She had to be talking about the Father of Cats.

"I was wondering why the woods were so quiet," the possum witch went on. "I haven't seen a cat all day. I thought L'il Pater might have been up to his tricks again."

"They did it to save my life," Lillian explained. "I was dying of a snakebite."

"Doesn't matter the reason. He's still not going to like it, and I really should get back to what I was doing."

"I can't stay like this," Lillian said, desperation flooding her voice.

"Why not?"

"It's not . . . natural. It's not who I am."

"You ought to have thought about that before you let them change you."

"I didn't know it was happening! I just woke up and I wasn't a girl anymore."

Old Mother Possum shook her head. "I can't help you with something like this."

"Why not?"

"I don't interfere with cat magic. That's some powerful mojo they've put on you. No wonder they're hiding. There's bound to be trouble when you take one natural creature and turn it into another."

"But can't you even try? I never asked to be a cat."

"First off," the possum witch told her, "if someone says they can't do something, it's not polite to press them on the whys and wherefores. Secondly, even if I could help you, I wouldn't. I value my own skin too much to get on the wrong side of that panther."

"It would just be setting things right again."

"Your mama let you backtalk her like that?"

Lillian couldn't help herself. All her kitten fur bristled.

"My mama's dead. The only kin I have is Aunt, and she's walking the woods right now, worried sick and looking for me."

"Then you'd better go to her," Old Mother Possum said. "Let her stop her worrying."

"I did. She doesn't recognize me like this."

Old Mother Possum sighed. "Well, I'm sorry you're in this predicament, but there's nothing I can do." She studied Lillian for a moment, then added, "And you'd do well to mind your manners. Next time you get pushy with someone they might not be as generous as I've been. Might be you'll find yourself in a situation you like even less than this one."

"I'm sorry," Lillian said, giving her paw a small lick.

Old Mother Possum nodded and turned away.

"I just wish none of this had ever happened," Lillian said. She was talking to herself now, but Old Mother Possum turned back and gave her a sharp look.

"You mean that?" she asked.

"Of course I do."

Old Mother Possum scratched at her chin again.

"Well, now," she said. "Let me think for a spell. Maybe I can help you with that. But you've got to be sure. Thing like that, it never works out quite the way you think it will."

"You can do that?" Lillian said. "You could make it like that snake never bit me?"

"Sure. That's easy. Takes about as much mojo as lighting a lamp with a snap of your fingers."

"Then could you do it for me?" Lillian asked, resisting an urge to weave back and forth against Mother Possum's legs. "Please?"

Old Mother Possum nodded. "But did you heed my warning? Thing like this, there's always some consequence or other tends to make a body less happy instead of more."

"Not me," Lillian said, shifting her weight from paw to paw. "I'd be very happy."

"Mm-hmm. Now, the way this works is you'll remember everything that happened, but nobody else will."

"That's fine. I need to remember so's to not let some awful snake bite me again."

"If you're sure . . ."

"Oh, I am, I am," Lillian said.

She wondered how it would work. She hoped she wouldn't have to drink some horrible potion. But all the possum witch did was snap her fingers, and the world went spinning away—

CHAPTER SIX

The Cat Who Woke Up as a Girl

And suddenly she was a girl again. The night and the swamp and the possum witch were all gone. It was the middle of the afternoon and she was running through a part of the woods that had been familiar until she'd followed the deer farther into them. She stumbled, thrown off balance by the sudden switch from four legs to two, but caught herself before she could fall. Her momentum carried her out from under the trees into a meadow.

And not just any meadow, she realized. The buck was no longer in sight, but there in the middle of an

expanse of grass and wildflowers was the ancient beech tree where she'd fallen asleep and gotten snakebit.

This time she knew enough not to lie down. No more snakebites for her, thank you very much.

"Hello hello!" she shouted to no one in particular. "I'm my very own self!"

She pulled a few daisies from their stems and tossed them in the air. It was so good to have hands

again. She did cartwheels all around the beech tree for the sheer joy of it. When she finally stopped to catch her breath, she leaned against the fat trunk of the beech and looked gingerly around her feet.

That hadn't been the smartest thing she'd ever done—turning cartwheels when she knew there was a nasty snake somewhere in the grass around the tree. But no matter how carefully she studied the grass and wildflowers, she couldn't see any sign of the snake.

Didn't mean it wasn't there, she thought.

But she had to wonder. The bite. The talking animals. The possum witch.

Had any of that really happened? Or had she fallen into some sort of storybook dream? That made a lot more sense. But if it had been a dream, how had she woken up running? Did people run in their sleep?

She decided it didn't matter. Not right now. Right now all she wanted to do was see Aunt and have Aunt recognize her.

With a lighthearted skip in her step, she set off for home.

$\sim$

Crossing the creek was easy now that she wasn't a cat. She ran through the woods, into the meadow, and up the hill. Her heart gave a little happy jump when she saw the roof of the barn, then the springhouse with the corncrib and the smokehouse behind it, and finally the old farmhouse itself.

She wanted to be turning cartwheels again, but they were too hard to do uphill. So she sang instead, a trilling *tra-la-la-la-la*. She could already imagine Aunt's face with the look that so plainly said, What's that silly girl up to now? But she didn't care because she was almost home again and everything was the way it was supposed to be.

Tra-la-la-la-la!

She saw Annabelle in the paddock and laughed, remembering how in her dream she'd imagined having a conversation with the cow. Cow and squirrel and crow and fox—it was all so silly. And the possum witch? Wherever had she come up with something like that?

"Hello hello, Annabelle!" she called as she skipped by the paddock. "Sorry—no time to talk!"

She laughed again as she made her way to the back of the farmhouse. As if a cow could talk. On the other side of the smokehouse she could hear Henry the rooster ordering the chickens around. She went up the stairs and into the summer kitchen, feet slapping on the wooden floor.

"Aunt!" she called. "Hello hello! I've had the strangest dream. You won't believe how harebrained it was. . . ."

Her voice trailed off when she realized she was talking to herself. Aunt wasn't in the kitchen. She wasn't in the parlor, either. Nor was she upstairs.

Had she said she was going to town, or to the Welches' farm? Lillian couldn't remember.

She leaned on the windowsill of her bedroom and looked out across the apple orchard, but there was nothing to see. A crow winged from the forest, banking on a breeze before it went gliding down toward the creek. She found herself wondering if it was Jack Crow, then smiled. Jack Crow wasn't real. He was just another part of her dream.

But the smile didn't seem to want to stick. Aunt being gone like this was worrisome.

Lillian turned from the window and went back downstairs. She made another circuit of the house before going outside once more. She looked in the corncrib and the smokehouse. She checked in the barn and the chicken coop. She walked past the beehives and up into the orchard, all the way to the family graveyard, then back down the hill again. Following the tree line, she stopped at the outhouse, calling for Aunt before she opened the door to peer in. The only thing inside was a spider, weaving its web in a corner.

"You should get packing," Lillian told the spider. "Aunt sees you settling in like that and she'll take a broom to you."

Aunt . . .

Lillian felt as though she had a big stone sitting in the bottom of her stomach.

"Oh, Aunt," she said as she turned away from the outhouse. "Where *are* you?"

She started back for the house, then changed direction as she realized the one place she hadn't looked was the small corn patch on the other side of the barn. She picked up her pace, calling for Aunt.

Her heart sank again as the patch came into view. The green corn was only up to her waist. If Aunt had been hoeing weeds between the rows, her tall, bony frame would have been easy to see. But there was no one there, either.

Lillian would have turned away, except just then she saw something odd down one of the rows. A smudge of gingham. Gingham like Aunt's dress.

She took a step closer, then she was running for where Aunt was lying in the dirt in between the rows of green corn.

"Aunt, Aunt!" she called out.

She wanted to pretend that Aunt was only lying down, having a rest, but she knew something was wrong. Something was terribly wrong. Stalks of corn were bent from where she'd fallen. Some were broken. Aunt lay with her face pressed into the ground, dirt smudged on her face.

Lillian dropped to her knees beside Aunt and gave her shoulder a little push.

"Get up, get up!" she cried. "Oh, please, get up."

But Aunt didn't move. And then Lillian noticed the two little marks on her ankle, surrounded by a red inflammation.

Snakebite.

No, no, *no*!

Surely Aunt had only fainted. In a moment her eyelids would flutter open and she would smile weakly at Lillian.

But no, this . . . this was different, and Lillian knew it. She was no stranger to death. She'd come across the remains of animals in the woods. She'd seen the cats kill mice and voles, spitting up a few tiny organs when they were done eating. She'd helped Aunt when one of the chickens was going to be dinner.

Lillian's chest felt like it might burst. This couldn't be true. Yet here was Aunt, lying gray-skinned on the ground.

She stroked Aunt's cooling brow and realized that her dream hadn't been some silly little thing she'd imagined. It had been a premonition. A warning. But it had come too late.

She lowered her head, pressing her face into Aunt's shoulder.

"Please wake up," she whispered. "Please, Aunt. I don't know what to do. . . ."

But she knew Aunt was gone. She cried for a long, long time.

~

Dusk was coming on when Lillian finally sat up. She sniffled and wiped her nose on the shoulder of her dress. Aunt was stiff now, her skin cold to the touch. Lillian was slow getting to her feet. She seemed to have no strength. All she had was what felt like a huge, gaping hole in the middle of her chest.

Oh, Aunt . . .

She was twice orphaned now.

Aunt had become her entire family—mother and father and every other relative you could have, all rolled up into one. Lillian didn't really remember her mother or father. Influenza had taken them when she was only a year old. The sickness had raged through the hills, and there was no rhyme nor reason why so many died, while others, such as Lillian and Aunt, were spared.

But now Aunt was gone, too.

Turning away, she shuffled through the rows of corn. When she got to the barn, she pulled an old blanket down from its peg and put it in the wheelbarrow. The wooden wheel rattled in its brackets as she left the barn and returned to the corn patch. But once she got the wheelbarrow in between the rows and into position, she couldn't lift Aunt onto the wooden slats of its bed. She wasn't nearly strong enough.

What was she supposed to do now? She couldn't just leave Aunt lying in the corn patch. What was going to happen? Why did she have to be so small and useless? Poor Aunt.

Kneeling in the dirt beside the wheelbarrow, her arms and shoulders aching from the effort, she started to cry again, but then quickly choked back her tears. If she let herself weep, she didn't think she'd ever be able to stop. There was still too much to do. She owed it to Aunt.

She sat up and gently laid the blanket over Aunt, then pushed herself to her feet. Her footsteps were heavy as she left the corn patch for a second time.

The hole in her chest felt even bigger—like nothing would ever fill it again.

It was almost full night now. She got Annabelle and brought her into the barn. Then she went to the house and got the lantern down from its shelf. Lighting the wick, she went outside. The lantern chased shadows away from her as she took the long path that led down to the Welches' farm.

CHAPTER SEVEN

Aunt's Gone

irdsong woke Lillian the next morning. She lifted her head in confusion, trying to figure out where she was, but then it all came flooding back. Her throat closed up and her eyes filled with tears. Sitting up, she wiped at them with a corner of the blanket.

The Welches' house was quiet. Glancing out the window, she saw that it was still very early. She got up and tiptoed into the kitchen, then out onto the porch. A barn cat jumped down from the railing, startling her. It gave her a long, thoughtful look, then slipped around the corner of the house. Lillian watched it go.

She thought about her strange dream: the circle of cats around the beech tree and the talking animals. The snakebite. She felt vaguely guilty, as though this were somehow her fault, that *she* should have been the snakebit one.

If only the dream *had* been real. She'd much rather be trapped in the shape of a cat if it meant that Aunt would still be alive.

She heard the door open behind her. Harlene joined her, putting an arm around Lillian's shoulders.

"How are you doing, hon?" she asked.

"I . . ." Lillian had to swallow hard before she could go on. "It . . . it doesn't feel real."

Harlene nodded. "It's going to be like that for a long time."

"But how will I manage without Aunt? Aunt was everything."

"I know. But we'll take good care of you. I promise."

This felt all wrong. *Aunt* took care of her. She and Aunt helped each other.

"I'd better go home," Lillian said. "I've got chores."

"No, you don't. Earl talked to the Creek aunts. A

couple of their boys are going to look after things for the next few days. We'll see what happens after that. You can't be living way up there all on your own, Lillian."

A shiver crawled up Lillian's spine. Leave the farm? The thought was unbearable, so she decided to ignore Harlene's last comment.

"What—what about Aunt?"

"Earl's gone into town to talk to the preacher. We'll lay her to rest with your mama and papa, up at the top of the hill. The Creek boys have offered to dig the grave."

"Where's Aunt now?"

"Earl said he laid her out in the parlor."

It had been a relief to let Harlene and Earl take over, but now Lillian felt totally powerless. She was like a leaf caught in an eddy, turning 'round and 'round alongside the shore.

She thought about poor Aunt lying all alone in the parlor.

"Can I go see her?" she asked.

"Of course you can, hon. I'll go up with you, and we can pick out something pretty for your Aunt Fran to wear. But before we go, I need to see to the livestock." She cocked her head. "Will you help?"

Lillian nodded. What else could she do?

~

The day they laid Aunt to rest started out sunny, but by the time they'd gathered in the small family plot on the hill above the Kindred farm, the skies had clouded over and threatened rain. Harlene and Earl Welch stood beside Lillian at the graveside. Lillian wore her good dress, and even had shoes on her feet. Preacher Bartholomew stood at the head of the grave, his Bible open in his hands.

A few other townsfolk and neighbors had made the long hike up to the farm. The Mabes, who lived a few farms over. Charley Smith from the general store. John Durrow and his son Jimmy, who grazed their cattle on the lower pastures near the road to town. Agnes Nash, who looked after the town's library. Humble Johnson, a banjo player who led the dances at the grange.

Standing behind them were the extended families of the Creeks—dark-skinned men in buckskin and denim, the women in long, embroidered black skirts, with their hair in braids. The aunts were in front, all except for Aunt Nancy, the oldest. She stood at the edge of the forest, half-hidden in shadow, her somber gaze never straying from Lillian.

At any other time her attention would have made Lillian nervous. No one knew Aunt Nancy's age. It was said that there'd been a Nancy Creek living in

these hills when the white men first came from the east and that she'd still be here long after they were gone. Lillian didn't know anything about that. She only knew that rowdy and joking though the Creek boys might be, they all grew quiet at even the mention of Aunt Nancy's name.

She didn't seem to be alone, standing there under

the trees. Lillian thought she could see
a dark figure standing behind her, even
taller than the stately Kickaha woman,
whose head was bowed in sorrow. It was
hard to tell, because she only stole
glances at them. Sometimes when she
looked the figure was there, sometimes it
was just Aunt Nancy.

Though the weight of the old woman's
gaze was heavy, it felt light compared
to the weight of Aunt's passing.

It had been hard for Lillian to look at Aunt laid out on the parlor table, hard when Samuel and John Creek lifted her into the coffin they'd built from scrap wood they'd found in the barn, harder still when they nailed shut the lid. Every bang of the hammer felt like a nail being punched into Lillian's chest.

And now the preacher was reading from his Bible, and soon they'd cover the coffin with dirt and Aunt would be gone forever. Her heart was breaking and her mind was spinning. She couldn't imagine what life was going to be like from here on out.

She couldn't concentrate on what the preacher was saying because it just felt senseless and empty. But when the brief ceremony was over, she stood tall, just like Aunt would have wanted her to, and accepted the condolences of the neighbors before they left.

The Creeks melted away into the forest, all except for Aunt Nancy, who lifted her hand and beckoned to Lillian with a long, dark finger. Harlene and Earl were talking in earnest to the preacher about something to do with Lillian, but they didn't even seem to think she should be part of the conversation. Relieved to get away, Lillian circled the grave and went to where Aunt Nancy stood.

The other figure was no longer there—if there ever had been anyone else standing behind Aunt Nancy. Perhaps she'd imagined it. Considering her dream—how real *it* had seemed—Lillian thought her imagination was much stronger than she wanted it to be.

"I'm sorry for your loss," Aunt Nancy said. "Your aunt was a good woman, and a good friend to my people. She will be missed."

Lillian nodded. "I don't know what I'm going to do without her."

Aunt Nancy's dark gaze rested on her for a long moment, and then something shimmered in her eyes, as though she were mildly startled.

"You know it doesn't have to be this way," she said.

Her voice seemed different—like it was coming from far away.

"P-pardon me? I don't understand," Lillian said.

"I think you do."

A hand fell on Lillian's shoulder before she could ask Aunt Nancy what she meant. She turned to see Earl behind her.

"What are you doing?" he asked.

"I was just . . ." Lillian began, turning back to Aunt Nancy, but there was no one there now. Talking to myself, she thought. "I was wondering why they all left so quickly," she finished. "The Creeks, I mean."

"You don't ever want to try to figure them out," Earl said. "It'll just make your head hurt. They may have been your aunt's friends, but they've always been a real strange bunch."

"I guess. . . ."

"Still, it was good of them to come by to pay their respects. And they've been a big help these past couple of days."

Lillian nodded.

Earl squeezed her shoulder.

"Come on," he said, steering her back toward the grave, where Harlene and the preacher waited. "We're going home now."

Home? Lillian thought. The Welches' farm wasn't her home. She glanced around, her heart filled with affection and sorrow. She was the last Kindred. *This* was her family home. But she let him lead her away.

As they followed the path back to the Welches' farm, Lillian trailed after the others, holding her shoes in her hand. She paused at the edge of her little family graveyard and turned to look back to the edge of the woods where the Creeks had stood. Something stirred in the undergrowth, and then Big Orange came out onto the grass. A half dozen other cats followed, with Black Nessie bringing up the rear. They sat in a ragged line, gazing in her direction. Lillian had the funny feeling that they were paying their respects, too.

She lifted a hand to them, but they didn't move. They were like a line of solemn little statues.

"Lillian?" Earl called.

At the sound of his voice the cats vanished like ghosts back in among the trees.

"I'm coming," she said.

As she followed the Welches and the preacher, she found herself thinking about what Aunt Nancy had said.

It doesn't have to be this way.

What had she meant?

Lillian worried the words forward and back as they made their way down the hill.

CHAPTER EIGHT

The Welch Farm

Lillian's first week at the Welch farm passed in a jumbled daze. All of Aunt's livestock—Annabelle, Henry, and the chickens—had been moved there, adding to a busy routine of chores. At least they helped distract her from her sorrow.

Lillian fed the chickens, tossing a little extra feed to the wild birds, just as she always did. There were pigs to look after, a garden to hoe and weed, horses to groom, and, of course, cows to milk and feed. She still set aside saucers for the forest cats.

But none of the cats came anywhere close to her now,

even though some, like Big Orange and Black Nessie, had followed her down from Aunt's. Naturally, the Welch farm cats were very shy of her—after all, they still had to get to know her. But strangely, the cats that she did know kept their distance as well. There were no more head butts from Big Orange, and Black Nessie didn't weave in and out around her legs anymore.

Something had changed. No, everything had changed. And Lillian had never felt more alone in her life.

Harlene tried hard—too hard—to make Lillian feel welcome. Her constant hovering, fixing favorite meals, offering to sew her a new dress, all of it just made Lillian miss Aunt, the farm, and her independence even more. All she wanted was to be back home at Kindred farm.

At first, Harlene had objected to letting her go off on her own after chores, but Lillian pointed out that it was what she had always done, and Earl finally said, "Stop trying to coddle the girl. She's not a prisoner." So Harlene compromised, saying Lillian could leave, but only if she took the dogs along for safety.

Lillian agreed to Harlene's rules—at least for now. She would have done anything to get back home, and anyway, Buddy and Mutt were good companions, always ready for a romp in the woods. More often than not she raced them all the way to the farm, just to feel the summer breeze in her hair and pretend for a moment that she was still a carefree little girl.

Sometimes she'd go to Aunt's vegetable garden and hoe between the rows.

She'd drop off a biscuit at the base of the Apple Tree Man's trunk, though she wasn't sure anymore if she did it out of habit, or because it was something Aunt used to tease her about.

But she never went into the corn patch.

Often, she thought about what Aunt Nancy had told her.

It doesn't have to be this way.

~

The wild cats watched her, always keeping their distance, even when the dogs were off chasing squirrels. They seemed to be wary of something, but Lillian had no idea what it could be.

She'd remember her dream then—that circle of cats around the beech tree—or she'd think of how they'd come to pay their respects at Aunt's funeral.

Those memories would make her begin to believe once again that the world was maybe a more mysterious place than a body might think.

~

Around the Welch farm, Harlene chattered and fussed, but Earl was all business. He didn't ignore

Lillian, but he didn't pander to her, either, for which she was grateful. Earl's conversations focused mostly around practicalities.

"A farm doesn't run by itself," he liked to say before attending to whatever task was at hand. One day he'd make sure the paddock was sound. Another, he might fix the rockwork around the well.

Lillian considered that as she went about her own chores.

One afternoon when she returned to Aunt's, she tried to look at the place with new eyes. She noted how the barn door sagged a little. Looking at the door and its hinges, she realized she didn't have the first idea of how to fix the sag. It wasn't a problem now, but come winter . . .

~

That night at the supper table she asked Earl if he'd teach her how to fix things around the farm. Earl smiled, but instead of answering straightaway, he looked over to Harlene.

"Well, you know, Lillian," Harlene said, "that's not something a lady needs to know."

Lillian gave her a puzzled look. "I'm not a lady."

"I know. You're just a girl now. But you're getting old enough that you need to start thinking about how you carry yourself. Just because your Aunt Fran had to run that whole place by her ownself doesn't mean you have to as well."

"But I *want* to. Aunt managed fine, and I can, too."

"Dear girl, you have no idea what you're saying. I don't know that we can find a body to buy that old farm of yours, it being so far from town and all, but I think we should start asking around."

"No!" Lillian blurted. Whatever was Harlene thinking?

But Harlene pressed on.

"In a few years you'll be wanting to catch the eye of some fine young man, and there's no meeting other people in these hills. You'll need some learning on how to be a proper young lady, not some barefoot tomboy, so you'd best be going to school in the fall."

"But I don't want to sell the farm, and I don't want go to school," Lillian said.

The idea of courting was too embarrassing to even mention.

"Everybody needs some learning. You want your

aunt to be proud of you, don't you, when she's looking down at you from Heaven?"

"I've been doing my lessons with Aunt," Lillian said.

"I know, hon. But Fran's not here anymore, and I'm no teacher."

Lillian didn't know what to say. It was bad enough that the snake had taken Aunt from her. Was it taking away her whole life now?

Tears brimmed in her eyes but she refused to cry.

"Harlene, go easy on the child. School's still the whole summer away," Earl said. "I don't see any harm in showing her a thing or two about looking after a farm until then."

Harlene frowned.

"Well, I don't," Earl said.

Lillian looked from one to the other. She knew something was happening, but she didn't know what. It seemed to lie under the words that the Welches were actually saying to each other—as though they were having two conversations at the same time.

"Fine," Harlene said after a moment. "But come the fall, she's going to school."

Don't I get any say in it? Lillian wondered, but she kept it to herself.

"Of course she'll go to school," Earl said, "but that doesn't mean she can't learn a few useful things in the meanwise."

Harlene gave a reluctant nod, and then turned to Lillian with a smile.

"Don't you worry," she said. "We'll raise you like you're our own daughter—just like your Aunt Fran would have wanted."

Lillian expected Harlene had that wrong. Aunt would never try to change Lillian into someone she wasn't.

But Harlene was right about one thing: Aunt wasn't here anymore. Harlene and Earl might be trying to look out for her, but they had their own notions as to who Lillian was and what she was supposed to become. And it wasn't going to matter one lick what Lillian herself thought about anything.

Now she guessed she understood a little better this business of two conversations going on at the same time. That was when you thought one thing, but you said something different.

Well, she could do that, too.

"I know you're looking out for me," she told Harlene, "and I appreciate it, I really do."

Harlene's smiled bright-
ened. "I know you do, hon.
You'll turn out to be the smartest young lady in the county. Just
you wait and see."

⌐

True to his word, Earl taught
Lillian to look for weaknesses in
structures and fences, and how to
mend them. As the summer wound
on, she became adept with a hammer and saw and
learned all the basic skills needed to keep Aunt's farm
running and in good repair.

She took pride in what she was learning, but she
couldn't exactly say she was happy. She didn't talk
about it, but she supposed they could see it on her face.

"A body can't depend on anybody else for their
happiness," Earl told her one day while they were re-
pairing the roof of the house. "The only way you can
ever find any peace is to find it in *yourself*—in what you
do and what you stand for."

Lillian wasn't sure what she stood for, but it didn't
include getting prissied up and going to school.

Only when she was away from the Welches' farm did she breathe easier. The woods seemed to open up and her footsteps were lighter. Even missing Aunt as much as she did couldn't stop the lift in her spirit.

Like the cats who watched and waited, she was waiting, too, only she wasn't quite sure for what.

～

Eventually, the days got shorter, dusk fell a little earlier every day, and that first day of attending classes was no longer a distant prospect.

Harlene remained fixed on the notion that there'd be some magical transformation when Lillian stepped across the threshold of the one-room school down the road. That Lillian would enter as a tomboy, but the moment she took her seat she'd be a proper young lady.

Lillian thought she might be able to stand wearing shoes all day, but she wasn't sure she could sit still for all that time. She liked learning. She enjoyed reading, knowing how to write was a good thing, and math was sort of interesting. She wouldn't mind being better at all of them.

But if she was in school all day, who would look after Aunt's farm? No one. It would only become one more abandoned homestead. And if it fell to ruin there'd be nothing of Aunt or the Kindred farm left in the world. No one would remember. No one would care.

Lillian couldn't let that happen. And that's when she understood what she had been waiting to do all this time.

The night before Harlene was to take her into town to buy a new dress, shoes, and school supplies, Lillian packed up her few belongings, left a note for Harlene and Earl, and walked back up into the hills. When she got to Aunt's farm, she stowed her bundle under the porch and then kept on going. The path she took now led east, deeper into the Tanglewood Forest.

CHAPTER NINE

Creek Boys

orty minutes later she reached her destination. From the tree line she could see the scattering of cabins in the hollow below. There were no lights on. Everybody was asleep, just as she should be.

She stepped off the path and found herself a nook in some tree roots. She planned to wait there until dawn, when the Creeks would be awake. But no sooner had she settled down than a voice called softly from the branches above.

"Hey, Lillian. What are you doing here?"

She started. For a moment she thought she was

back in her dream, where birds and animals talked
to her from out of the trees. But then she recognized
the voice. She peered up into the branches and could
make out the dark shape of John Creek sitting on a
bough.

"Hello hello," she said. "I could ask you the same
thing."

John swung down from the branch and dropped lightly onto the ground.

"I'm just fooling around with Davy," he said. "We're having a contest to see who can—"

He broke off when a stick hit his shoulder.

"Gotcha!" Davy cried.

He stepped out from the underbrush on the other side of the path, tall and dark-haired like all the Creek boys.

"No fair," John said. "I'm having a time-out talking to Lillian."

"You didn't call time-out! Hello, Lillian."

Lillian nodded to him. "So the two of you are running around in the middle of the night playing tag?"

John shrugged. "It's more fun at night, when everybody else is asleep."

"When it's just us," Davy added, then switched to a spooky voice, "and . . . *the spirits.*"

John immediately took up Davy's teasing.

"And a lot of them," he whispered, "are not happy to have us out here in the woods with them, disturbing their—you know, whatever it is that spirits do."

Davy punched him in the shoulder. "Way to mess it up."

The two boys laughed and Lillian had to smile.

"Do you want to play?" Davy asked.

Lillian shook her head.

"Why are you hiding here?" John asked. "Are you spying on us?"

"No, I'm here to see Aunt Nancy."

The boys exchanged nervous looks.

"Are you sure you want to do that?" John said.

Davy nodded. "Yeah, nobody just decides to see Aunt Nancy. We only go to her when she sends for us."

"Especially these days," John added. "She's been in a mood."

"She said something to me at the funeral," Lillian said, "and I need to ask her what she meant by it."

"What did she say?"

"'It doesn't have to be this way.' What do you suppose she meant by that?"

The boys shook their heads.

"Well," Lillian said, "don't you feel like everything just seems a little . . . *wrong* these days?"

They shook their heads again.

"Maybe," Davy said, "you're just feeling that way because of your Aunt Fran having passed and all."

John nodded. "I remember when Uncle Sammy passed last year. We all missed him something fierce."

"It's not just me missing Aunt—I do miss her terrible—but I've had this bad feeling all summer. The wild cats are always looking at me and looking at me, watching everything I do like they expect me to sprout a third arm or something. I need to see if Aunt Nancy can help me."

The boys exchanged concerned looks.

"I'd be careful," John said. "The spirits start paying more attention to folks who come 'round to see Aunt Nancy."

"Yeah," Davy added, "and it's never a good idea to have the spirits pay attention to you. They're not like you or me. They'll as soon drop the world from under your feet as do you a favor. You just never know."

Lillian smiled. "Here we go again."

"No," John told her. "We were fooling with you before. This is different. Aunt Nancy is serious."

"And like John said, she's been in a mood."

Lillian kept up her brave face.

"I still have to talk to her," she said. "I have to do *something*. I can't turn into this prim little doll that

Harlene thinks I should be. She wants me to get all prissied up and go to school. That's just not me."

Davy cocked his head. "I wonder how you'd look, all cleaned up and girly?"

John gave him a push.

"Knock it off," he said. "This is serious." He turned to Lillian. "Maybe Aunt Nancy just meant you could come live here with us."

"Or maybe," Davy said, "she wants you to 'prentice with her. She's never chosen anybody to take her place for when she moves on."

"That's because she's not going anywhere," John said. "She's been around forever. She'll probably be around forever."

Lillian gave him a puzzled look. "You don't believe that old story, do you?"

"I know how it sounds," John said, "but my granddad told me she's the same today as when he was a boy, and his granddad told him the same."

"That's not possible."

"No," Davy agreed. "That's Aunt Nancy."

"She's not even a full-blooded Kickaha," John went on. "Did you know that?"

Lillian shook her head.

"Her daddy came from Africa, I heard—long before the slaves were brought here."

"Why do you say she's in a mood?" Lillian asked.

Davy shrugged. "Who knows?"

"You can't stay out here all night," John said. "Come back to my place. Annie's sleeping over at Pieta's, so you can have her bed."

"What's your mama going to say?"

"Nothing. We'll tell her in the morning and she'll just set out another plate for breakfast. Then you can go see Aunt Nancy—which I still don't recommend."

Lillian nodded. But she saw another problem now. "If the Welches come looking for me," she said, "you can't let on I'm here."

"Don't worry about that," Davy said. "We all like Harlene and Earl just fine, but once everybody knows you've got business with Aunt Nancy, they'd sooner suck on a rotten egg than talk about it to anybody."

"Yeah," John said. "Nobody's dumb enough to get mixed up in Aunt Nancy's business unless they don't have a choice."

Lillian let the boys lead her down the hill to John's house.

"You've got to feel a little sad for Aunt Nancy," she said.

John gave her a puzzled look.

"Well, think about it. Everybody's so scared of her, she's got no friends."

John nodded. "I see what you mean. But you know, I think she's got friends—we just can't see them. I've walked by her cabin and heard her talking away when I know there's no one else there. Leastwise nobody I ever saw go in."

Lillian shivered. Maybe going to talk to Aunt Nancy wasn't such a good idea, but Lillian *had* to find out what she meant. It was her only shred of hope for finding a way to have the life she wanted.

"You want to come in now?" John asked.

Lillian nodded.

CHAPTER TEN

Aunt Nancy

John's mother didn't seem at all surprised to see Lillian the next morning. As John had said, she simply laid out another plate and asked her how she'd slept. Creek children—ranging in age from toddlers to John's older brother Samuel, who was almost eighteen—filled the kitchen with a happy clamor.

"Are you *really* going to see Aunt Nancy?" Samuel asked. "On purpose?"

"Samuel!" his mother said.

He shrugged. "I'm just asking."

All the Creek children stopped eating and stared wide-eyed at Lillian to see what she would say.

Lillian played self-consciously with the food on her plate, pushing scrambled eggs and bacon around with her fork. A big knot of fear was lodged in her stomach, and none of this was helping. She managed to take a bite of fry bread before she stood up from the table.

"I should go," she said. "I'm sorry I'm not hungry, but thanks for breakfast, Mrs. Creek."

"My pleasure, dear. I hope everything goes well with Aunt Nancy."

Lillian hesitated. "Why's everybody so scared of her?"

"Well, now. I have to admit she can be a trial from time to time, but she's never hurt a body that didn't deserve to be taken down a peg or two. Just be polite, and I'm sure you'll be fine."

Easy to say, Lillian thought, when it's not you going to see her.

She thanked John's mother again and went outside. John had already pointed out to her Aunt Nancy's cabin, which stood a little distance from the others. It was a pine-log structure with a cedar-shingle roof and a small porch out front. A pair of towering sprucy-pine stood tall on either side. Bundles of drying herbs hung from the porch rafters, and a big black cat the size of a bobcat lay at the top of the stairs, staring right at her the way all the cats seemed to these days, like it was anticipating something.

That made it no easier, but she started for the cabin with her knees knocking and her heart pounding. She stopped with a jump when she heard Davy shout her name.

"The Welches are up at the farm looking for you," he yelled as he ran over from the path that led to Aunt's farm.

"Did you say anything to them?"

He gave her a withering look. "They never even knew I was there."

"What were they doing?"

"Looking around, calling your name."

"Do you think they'll come here?" she asked.

"Probably."

"Well, thanks for letting me know."

She squared her shoulders and started back toward Aunt Nancy's cabin.

"You're *really* going to just knock on her door?" Davy asked.

"Please, Davy," Lillian said over her shoulder. "Let it be. I need to see her."

Davy shrugged. "I'll come by later and pick up the pieces," he called after her.

Lillian didn't bother to answer. As she approached the stairs the big cat stood and arched its back before turning and leaping onto the other end of the porch rail.

"Pleased to meet you, too," Lillian said as she edged her way up the stairs. Rubbing her hands together, she took a deep breath, then knocked on the door. There was no response. Lillian turned to look at Davy, who stood right where she'd left him, hands in his pockets. She was about to knock on the door again when it jerked open and there stood Aunt Nancy, tall and formidable.

"It's you," Aunt Nancy said.

Lillian cleared her throat, but before she could speak Aunt Nancy went on: "I should have realized when I saw you at the funeral. What have you *done*?"

"I didn't—I mean, I never—"

"There are always consequences," Aunt Nancy said. "Why can't anyone remember that?" Her gaze went past Lillian to where Davy was standing. "Do you need something from me, Davy Creek?"

"N-no, ma'am."

"Then why are you standing there? If you've nothing to do, I can find you a few chores."

"I think I hear my dad calling me," Davy said.

He jogged away and Aunt Nancy returned her attention to Lillian.

"You'd better come inside," she said.

That was the last thing Lillian wanted to do. She didn't know what Aunt Nancy thought she'd done, but she knew it wasn't good.

"Well?" Aunt Nancy said. "I don't have all day to dawdle out here."

Lillian went inside, each step more reluctant than the one before.

Aunt Nancy's cabin was clean and tidy, as opposed to the happy chaos of the one where John lived. More herbs hung from the inside rafters, but as clean as the rest of the cabin was, there were masses of cobwebs up in the ceiling corners. Lillian pretty much loved anything that walked or flew or swam, including spiders, but those cobwebs gave her the creeps.

Aunt Nancy motioned her to a wooden-backed chair at the small kitchen table and sat down across from her. She folded her hands on the polished pine surface of the table and regarded Lillian with her dark gaze.

"Tell me what you did," she said, "and maybe we can fix it."

"Do—do you mean my running away from the Welches'?" Lillian tried.

"That depends. When was that?"

"Last night."

Aunt Nancy shook her head. "No, things have been going wrong since long before that. Haven't you felt it?"

Lillian could barely think. This wasn't going well at all. She knew several things felt wrong, but they all had to do with losing Aunt and her old life. None of them seemed like anything *she'd* done.

"Well, it's not your running away," Aunt Nancy said without waiting for her reply. "But I trust my bones. I can sense that day by day the world is going someplace it shouldn't, and as soon as I found you standing there on my porch, I could see that you're smack dab in the middle of it all. So I'll ask you again: What. Have. You. Done?"

Lillian felt a pang of guilt in the pit of her stomach. She must have done *something*, elsewise Aunt Nancy wouldn't be pointing the finger at her. And what about the cats, always watching from a distance? What made them so wary of her?

Cats . . . her strange dream about the snakebite and the cats' magic. Could it have something to do with that? No, surely a dream wouldn't count, and she didn't want to make Aunt Nancy angry by mentioning anything so silly.

"I honestly didn't do anything."

"But maybe something happened close to you? It would have been around the beginning of the summer."

"I can't think of anything except for Aunt dying," Lillian said. "After her funeral you said, 'It doesn't have to be this way.' What did you mean?"

"I said those words?"

Lillian nodded. "That's why I came to see you."

"That's strange," Aunt Nancy told her. "I don't remember that at all, and I remember everything. Unless . . ."

Her voice trailed off.

"Unless what?" Lillian asked.

"Sometimes the spirits speak through me," Aunt Nancy explained, "but unfortunately, only those around me can hear what they have to say. I don't even know it's happened unless someone tells me." She gave Lillian a rueful smile. "And since most folks avoid me, they don't think to mention it."

"The spirits," Lillian repeated. "What would spirits want with *me*?"

"I don't know. But now you see that, clearly, what-ever's going on has something to do with you."

"There's maybe one thing, but . . ."

"Stop playing coy and tell me what happened."

"Well . . . would a dream count?" Lillian asked.

Aunt Nancy gave her a considering look.

"What kind of dream?"

"A strange one. Sort of like a fairy tale or a . . . premonition."

"Tell me."

"But it was just a dream."

"Dreams can be potent," Aunt Nancy said. "Tell me what you remember of it."

"I remember everything," Lillian said.

And she did, so it took a while to tell. She started with how she'd gone chasing after the deer, and fin-ished up with the possum witch sending her back.

"So I guess I was sleeprunning," she finished, "though I've never heard of such a thing before. But I woke up running, and the next thing I knew, I came to that same beech tree in its glade, but there weren't any cats there. No snake, neither—not that I could see. That didn't come until later, when . . . when

I found Aunt in the corn patch. But you see what I mean about it feeling like a premonition?"

Aunt Nancy nodded. But instead of commenting on the dream, she said, "I've heard there was a possum witch in these hills, but I didn't know where."

Lillian stared at her with wide eyes.

"You mean . . . Was it all *real*?"

"Now, how would I possibly know a thing like that?" Aunt Nancy asked.

"But if the possum witch is real . . ."

"Hard to tell. Every dream doesn't spell out a piece of the future. I just meant it was curious, is all."

"I don't understand."

"Well, you said you'd never heard tell of a possum witch, but there you were, dreaming of one all the same."

"So what does it mean?"

Aunt Nancy shook her head. "It feels like there's something from the long ago sticking its nose here in our business, but it comes from so far back that I can't get a proper fix on it. Just sit quiet for a spell. Let me try to hear what this old spirit is telling me."

Curious as she was, Lillian had been warned many times in her life that it was unwise to attract the attention of the spirits, so she looked anywhere but directly at Aunt Nancy, who'd fallen into a trance. Lillian glanced all around the cabin, but her gaze kept going to those huge cobwebs, which made her shudder. What were they doing there?

Aunt Nancy made no sound, but her lips moved silently from time to time, as though in conversation. Finally, she opened her eyes and fixed her gaze on Lillian.

"You've been through a lot, child, but your trials are not over."

Lillian took a big breath, then let it out. "I'm ready to do anything to make things go back to the way they were before Aunt died."

Aunt Nancy nodded. "As I said, your trials are not over. The spirits say you need to go to the bear people. Maybe they can help you sort this dream out."

Lillian didn't like the sound of that. She'd come here hoping for a solution to her problems, not more mysteries.

"What? I thought the spirits said they could help me."

"Do not disrespect me or the spirits, Lillian, or you will have more problems than you could ever bargain for. You must go to the bear people to find answers."

"Are they another tribe—like the Kickaha?"

"Depends on what you mean by *tribe*. I think of them as a very old tribe, but they are not exactly people."

"What do you mean, not exactly people?" Lillian asked.

"Only that they go back to what the first people call the long ago, when the world was new. People weren't so settled into their shapes in those days."

"Are they friendly?" Lillian asked.

"Their people and ours don't really get along," Aunt Nancy said. "A long time ago we hunted them for their fur and meat. But they may be friendly to you."

"You *ate* them?"

"Not when they were people. Nobody living on the rez today has ever hunted them. But memories are long, especially among the old tribes. You'll need to go to them on your own."

"I don't understand why the spirits said 'It doesn't have to be this way,' and now you're sending me all by myself to meet some long-lost enemy."

"I told you not to question the advice of the spirits, young lady. One of the boys can take you to where the rez ends, but after that, yes, you'll have to go alone."

"What if they eat me?"

"They probably won't."

"Probably?"

Aunt Nancy nodded. "I suggest you approach them with respect."

Lillian sighed. Why does everybody always assume I'm going to be rude? she thought.

"So I'm supposed to go see these bear people," Lillian said, "and if they don't eat me, they might help me."

"No one's making you go."

"It looks like I don't have any other choice," said Lillian.

Aunt Nancy nodded. "You need to fix this thing, or it's only going to get worse." She stood up from the table, adding, "I'll find someone to get you on your way."

CHAPTER ELEVEN

Holes
in the Sky

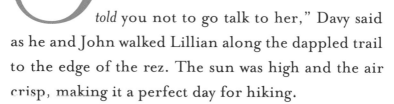

told you not to go talk to her," Davy said as he and John walked Lillian along the dappled trail to the edge of the rez. The sun was high and the air crisp, making it a perfect day for hiking.

Lillian carried a blanket roll on her back, plus a canteen and a small shoulder bag with some food that Mrs. Creek had packed for her: apples and cheese, a couple of fresh fry breads. The boys walked on either side, plying her with questions, while lanky rez dogs ranged ahead under the canopy of the trees. Lillian had tried to satisfy the boys' curiosity as best she could with a shortened version of her story.

John nodded. "I'll admit that's one crazy dream of yours, but I don't see how it could be real. And all because of that you're going off to get eaten by a bear."

"I'm not going to be eaten by a bear," Lillian said, feigning a courage that she didn't feel.

"Seems like it to me," Davy said, "which makes me wonder why Aunt Nancy's sending you to them. I used to think she had a soft spot for you and your aunt."

"It's not really Aunt Nancy's doing," Lillian told them. "The spirits told her I should go."

"Sure, but—"

"Anyway, they're supposed to be some kind of bear *people*. Not bears for real. They wouldn't just up and eat me."

"Well," John said, "I guess we never told you the story about how stars are the holes left in the sky from when the spiders dropped down."

"I guess you never did."

John stopped in his tracks and dropped down to the ground, sitting cross-legged in the grass. Davy followed suit. Lillian hesitated, then sat down in front of them. The dogs came back and sprawled in a loose circle around them.

"This happened a long time ago," John said, "back when the bears lived more like bears than like people. That might seem a strange way to put it, but back then there weren't many humans, so the animal people mostly just walked around in their animal skins. Anyway, they were going about their business when along comes this little girl.

"The bears didn't know what to make of her, so they put her in the bottom of a natural well out in front of their caves while they figured out what to do. It was a deep, deep well, dark down there at the bottom where the little girl was stuck, with smooth sides going all the way up so she couldn't climb out. But

she could see a little circle way up that she knew was the sky, and she could hear the bear people talking. When they finally decided that they might as well just eat her, she knew she was in real trouble."

"What did she do?" Lillian had to ask.

John smiled. "Well, what the bears didn't know was that the little girl was the daughter of the great spider spirit. When Old Man Night finally rolled his big black blanket across the sky, she called out to all the little spider spirits that make their homes in the dark, dark wool of Old Man Night's blanket. Answering her call, they dropped down from the sky in the thousands, and every place they dropped from, there was a little hole left behind that we still see in the night skies to this day.

"But that night they wove their webs and made a ladder so that the little girl could climb out of the well, and they wrapped all the sleeping bears in their webs so that they couldn't move. They couldn't even breathe.

"Then the little girl ate them, one by one."

"She ate them all?" Lillian asked.

John nodded.

"Oh, she was mad, mad, and she would've eaten

every one, except for a couple had been off hunting and spent the night in a cave. Imagine coming home to *that*."

He looked around carefully, as though he was afraid of being overheard, then leaned in closer to Lillian.

"I've heard tell," he said in a soft voice, "that Aunt Nancy was that same little girl, and she's still mad at those bears."

Lillian's eyes opened wide. "Really?"

"Did you ever see all those spiderwebs up in the rafters of her cabin?"

"Yes, but—"

Then she caught the flicker of a smile in the corner of John's mouth.

"Oh, you!" she cried, and punched him in the shoulder.

John and Davy fell back on the grass, laughing. The dogs jumped up and ran around in circles, barking.

"I still don't see what any of that's got to do with me," Lillian said when things had calmed down.

Davy's eyebrows rose. "You mean besides being a little girl walking up to a cave full of bears and asking them for their advice?"

"You can try and scare me," Lillian told him, "but Aunt Nancy was mostly pretty nice to me. She's stern and kind of spooky, but she's not really mean."

"I suppose that's true," John said with a grin. "Especially the stern and spooky part."

Lillian ignored his tease. "Talking to these bear people's the only thing anyone's said might help me," she said. "And when was the last time you heard about a bear going after somebody unless they got between a mother and her cubs? It's not like the bears in these hills are all fierce the way grizzlies are supposed to be."

"Maybe so," Davy said, "but I still wouldn't be doing it."

They hiked on for a while, kicking up fallen pine needles as they followed the trail through a section of sprucy-pine forest. Cantankerous squirrels scolded them from the safety of tree boughs, but the three paid them no mind.

Once Lillian thought she caught a glimpse of Big Orange watching them from the top of a ridge, but John said it was just a fox, adding, "He's lucky the dogs didn't catch wind of him."

After a while they came out from under the woods

into a wide meadow that stretched to the far tree line in waves of golden-brown grass and purple asters. A crow croaked from the trees behind them before it sailed over the meadow. Lillian watched it vanish into the tops of the tall sprucy-pine.

When they reached the far side of the meadow the boys stopped. The dogs came back, pushing muzzles against their legs as if to ask, What's the holdup?

"This is as far as we can go," Davy said.

"We'd come all the way," John said, "but when

Aunt Nancy lays down the law, you do what she says
or she'll tan your hide."

"That's all right," Lillian told them. "Thanks for
taking me this far."

John nodded. "Keep going north till you come to
a rocky ridge, then follow it down to the creek below.
If you stay near the creek, it'll take you back up into
the hills again. You'll see caves under a big overhang,
and I guess that's as good a place as any to start looking for bears."

"It'll probably take you most of the day to get there," Davy added, "so you'll maybe want to hole up somewhere before the sun sets. If you're going to meet a bear, I expect it'll be more comfortable in the morning than at night."

"I expect it will," Lillian said with a tremor in her voice.

She thanked them again, then set off before she lost her nerve completely. When she looked back a little later, the boys and dogs were gone. In their place was a row of cats, sitting on deadfalls and stumps and the ground, watching her.

CHAPTER TWELVE

The Hunter

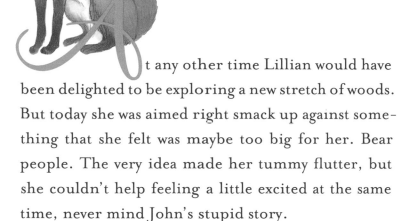

At any other time Lillian would have been delighted to be exploring a new stretch of woods. But today she was aimed right smack up against something that she felt was maybe too big for her. Bear people. The very idea made her tummy flutter, but she couldn't help feeling a little excited at the same time, never mind John's stupid story.

She followed a deer trail through the autumn woods, admiring the colorful foliage and thinking about having crafted grapevine-and-leaf wreaths with Aunt last fall. She hoped that the bear people would be able to set things right.

It felt good to have a sense of purpose. It had been a long stretch of whenever since she'd felt she was doing more than just getting through a day. Maybe she ought to have gone to see Aunt Nancy a lot sooner.

The land rose slowly toward to the ridge that John had told her to look for. Oak and beech gave way to sprucy-pine. Under their tall spreading boughs there was less undergrowth, and her lone footsteps crunched noisily on the carpet of needles. Mushrooms sprouted from deadfalls, alone and in clusters: red and white, bright yellow, mustard yellow. The bare granite bones of the land pushed up out of the ground in ever-larger formations.

It was only when she reached the top of the ridge that she realized she was being followed.

At first she thought it was one of the Creek boys, planning to play another trick on her. Davy or John, or maybe both of them. She kept turning casually, hoping to catch them at their game, but they were good at hiding. Then she thought it was the cats again, except they never bothered to hide from her. When she finally did catch a glimpse of her pursuer, it was a flash of russet fur darting behind a stone outcrop.

She stopped in her tracks, staring at the place where the fox had disappeared. A memory popped into her mind, and for a moment she couldn't remember if it was a real memory or if it had come from the strange dream she'd had the day Aunt died. But then she had to laugh at herself.

T. H. Reynolds, the *talking* fox? Of *course* he was from her dream. But it was confusing the way the idea of impossible things kept tumbling into the real world. Once upon a time she would have been delighted with the idea of talking foxes or bear people, but she wasn't the little girl chasing fairies in the meadow anymore. And never mind what Aunt Nancy had told her, she suspected that the bear people would just be some hermit clan living deep in the hills. Strange, to be sure, but quite human.

She set off again, following the ridge, picking her way around the stone outcrops and tree roots. And while it made little sense, she kept catching glimpses of the red fox sneaking along behind her. She knew that sometimes wild critters just got curious. And sometimes they were sick. Rabies could make even a

squirrel do things it would never do otherwise—like follow a girl much bigger than itself.

Whyever this fox was following her, it was creepy. And she was fed up with it.

Picking up a good-sized stick, she held it in a tight grip and glared at the last place she'd seen the fox dart out of sight.

"All right, Mr. Fox," she called out to it. "Or maybe you really are T. H. Reynolds. I don't know and I don't care. But you need to either stop following me or step out where I can see you."

She wasn't actually expecting a response, so when a voice spoke to her from the branches of the tree above her, she thought her heart would stop.

"Hey, little missy. Think you could keep it down?"

She felt as though she'd fallen back into her dream again, where creatures kept talking to her from trees. Looking up, she half expected to see the fox sitting up there on a branch—or at least Jack Crow.

The foliage was thick, and at first she didn't see anyone. Then a shadow shifted, moving into a shaft of light, and she saw that there was a man up in the tree. He had a long face with a raggedy beard and a wrinkled brown hat pushing down on top of a mass of straggly hair. His rangy frame was tucked into a crook between a couple of big branches and the trunk. A rifle lay across his knees.

"What are you *doing* up there?" Lillian asked, too surprised to be scared.

"Well, I was hunting until you came traipsing down the ridge making enough noise for a whole herd of little girls. Any game for a mile around is going to have been scared away."

"I wasn't making that much noise."

"Oh, no? You walk like you weigh ten times your size. And then there was all that shouting. Somebody should have told you before this that a fox isn't going to be tracking some little girl, and he sure enough isn't going to answer your questions."

Lillian flushed. All the fancies that the Creeks had put in her head washed away and she felt like a fool.

"I *know* that," she said.

"Do you now."

Lillian gave him a determined nod and changed the subject.

"What are you hunting?"

"I've got my sights set on a big panther. I've seen

him a time or two and decided to see if I can track him down. That pelt of his'll fetch a handsome price."

Maybe it was all dreams and fancies, but Lillian couldn't help thinking about the things Jack Crow had told her.

"Do you mean the Father of Cats?" she almost whispered.

The man shrugged. "Well, now, he sure looks big and old enough to have been around since the beginning of time. But this isn't some parlor-story fairy-tale cat. It's just an any-old-day panther that keeps coming around my farm, looking to get at the calves."

"You've really seen him?"

"I catch me a glimpse, time to time, but I never can get me a shot. He's smart, that cat. Been around awhile—you can tell. But I can be patient."

"Where's your farm?" Lillian asked, wondering if he might know about the bear people.

He jerked his chin to the west, rather than north.

"Over yonder," he said. "A couple of miles as the crow flies." He chuckled. "Takes me a little longer to make the trip."

"Do you ever see any bear around here?"

He shook his head. "I know there's some higher

up in the hills, but they don't much come down my way—leastwise, I don't see any sign. Doesn't really surprise me since there's nothing for them. I don't have an orchard or beehives or even a berry patch."

Lillian couldn't think of a way to ask about bear people without feeling more ridiculous.

"Well," she said, "I've still got a-ways to go, so I guess I'll be seeing you."

"You never did say why you're up this far into the hills."

Lillian gave him a bright smile. "Talking to foxes," she said.

"Ha, ha. But seriously, you're awful young to be out on your own, this deep in the hills. Where do you live?"

Nowhere, Lillian thought. She didn't have a home anymore. At least not until she figured out how to save Aunt's farm. But that wasn't anything she was about to tell a stranger.

"Back there a-ways," she said, pointing.

Then she waved a hand and set off at a jaunty pace that wasn't anything like she felt.

"You be dang careful!" the hunter called after her.

She waved again but didn't look back.

Lillian expected the hunter to come down from his perch to follow after her, which would make him yet one more person who felt he should get to decide what she was supposed to do with her life. But she didn't hear any ruckus. When she finally did hear something behind her a few minutes later, a quick glance showed her the plume of a fox's tail disappearing behind a bush.

"Fine," she said, "Go ahead and skulk along behind me. See if I care."

She looked up in the tree she was passing under, half expecting someone to be sitting up there. Another hunter. Maybe some fairy-tale creature. *Somebody* with something to say that she didn't particularly want to hear.

But the branches were empty, which made perfect sense. Hunters were busy with their own lives, and her life wasn't a fairy tale. It was a sad mess and there wasn't anything magical about it. There wasn't anything magical anywhere at all.

Yes, Aunt Nancy was fairly spooky, but really. *Bear people?*

She stopped and sat down on the long trunk of

a fallen tree, ready to retrace her steps. Except that wouldn't help, either. The Welches and school were waiting for her back there.

And going ahead would—what?

Well, it might get her eaten by a bear. Or a panther . . .

She sighed and looked back the way she'd come.

"What do you think, Mr. Fox?" she called to the empty woods. "Do you have any advice for me?"

Of course there was no reply.

~

Lillian went on despite her reservations. The game trail she followed through the sprucy-pine wound its

way in between tree trunks and stone outcrops soft-
ened with moss. She walked along the back of the
ridge for miles, weariness starting to set in just when
the ground started to rise again.

Hunger pangs reminded her that she'd skipped
breakfast, and she was grateful that there was food in
her pack. She stopped by a jumble of rock to have
some cheese and fry bread, washing it down with water. When she was rested enough to continue, she
stood up and left a small portion of cheese on the
stone where she'd been sitting.

"That's for you, Mr. Fox," she said.

She hadn't seen him for a while so she wasn't even sure he was still on her trail.

Curiosity got the better of her, and thirty feet or so from where she'd left the cheese she ducked behind a big mossy stone, then slowly rose until she could peer over the top. She stayed as still as ever she had and, sure enough, a few minutes later the fox stepped into sight on dainty feet, his plume of a tail lifting behind him. He sniffed at the food, then snapped it up in one bite. His head came up and he looked around until his gaze found hers. She ducked down. When she looked back a moment later, he was gone.

~

The trail wound up the mountain until it finally opened into a small meadow. The afternoon was slipping away and she remembered Davy's advice about finding a place to spend the night.

She crossed the meadow and the trail began its descent once more. The incline was steep and she had to hold on to saplings as she went down. As twilight finally crept over the forest she came to a small creek. A tall pine had recently fallen, forming a bridge across the water. She drank from the creek and filled her canteen, then crossed over. She walked the length of the pine until it grew too narrow.

Follow the creek, John had told her. Well, she'd do that tomorrow.

Hopping down, she made herself a nest under the pine boughs. She rolled out her blanket and lay down. She thought about the fox and the hunter and the bears she might or might not meet tomorrow. Finally the long day caught up with her, and she fell fast asleep.

CHAPTER THIRTEEN

Mother Manan

When Lillian woke it was morning. She looked up through the pine boughs and smiled to hear the bird chorus. The scent of pine and the forest loam upon which she lay filled her nose, and for a long moment she was able to forget why she was out here in the forest.

Stretching lazily, she slipped out from under the fallen pine, pulling her gear after her. There was still plenty of water in her canteen, and the creek was only a hop, a skip, and a jump away, but her food sack was woefully lighter than it had been when

Mrs. Creek had given it to her. She rolled up her blanket and tied it with her carrying strap. It was only when she turned around that she discovered she was no longer alone.

A few feet away from where she'd slept under the boughs of the fallen pine was the biggest man she'd ever seen.

At first glance she thought he was pretty much as wide as he was tall, but then she realized he was crouched down. Standing up he'd be bigger still— seven, maybe eight feet tall, towering over her like the sprucy-pine and oak. His beard and hair were a reddish-brown tangle that bushed up around his face like a cluster of thornbushes around an apple tree. He was dressed in a collection of furs and linen scraps, all sewn together in a haphazard fashion.

She couldn't tell how old he was, only that he wasn't as old as Aunt had been, nor as young as she was. He was somewhere in the long distance in between. She couldn't tell his mood, either. His dark brown eyes studied her without blinking, and she found herself unable to breathe until he finally spoke.

"There's something unnatural about you, little girl," he said, his voice a low rumble that seemed

to reverberate in her chest. "Who are you and what are you hiding?"

"I—my name's Lillian."

"Hmm."

"And I don't know what you mean."

He gave a slow nod. "People say that when they have something to hide."

"Well, that wouldn't be me."

"What are you doing in my hills?"

"Your " Lillian began, but her voice trailed off as she finally realized who this must be. "I'm looking for the bear people."

"And why would you be doing a thing like that?"

"Aunt Nancy told me I should. She's—"

Something darkened in the man's eyes. "We know who *she* is. What does she want from us?"

"So you *are* one of the bear people?"

"Patience, little girl. *I'm* asking the questions here. Tell me, why did Nancy Creek send you here?"

Lillian wanted to crawl back under the pine and curl up into a ball. Anything to get away from the bear man's hostile gaze and cross tone.

"She—she said you might be able to interpret my dream."

"Did she now."

It didn't sound like a question, but Lillian nodded in response all the same.

The bear man studied her again. When he finally stood, he seemed to rise up forever. Lillian thought he might be even more than eight feet tall.

"You're coming with me," he said. "We'll see what Mother Manan has to say about this story of yours. But I can tell you this much: Your being a spy for Nancy Creek won't stand in your favor."

"I'm not a spy," Lillian said. "She scares me a little, too."

He snorted. "What makes you think she scares me?"

"Nothing. I just find her scary, so I figure everybody does."

Lillian was afraid of the bear man as well, but she wasn't going to tell him that. She probably didn't have to. All he had to do was look at how her knees were knocking against each other.

"You know," she said, "if your mother's not going to help me, maybe I should go home and not waste everybody's time."

He smiled but his eyes narrowed.

"No," he said, "you'll be coming with me. The

question is, will you walk or will I have to carry you under my arm?"

~

It wasn't a long hike to where the bear people lived, but it seemed long to Lillian as she tramped along beside the enormous man. He hadn't come right out and threatened her, but his attitude filled her with dread. Was she his walking dinner?

She kept sneaking glances at him. It was like walking beside a giant, except he had a softer step than she did. Maybe the hunter she'd met yesterday was right. She did walk like a whole crowd of little girls.

Finally they came through a narrow cleft in the rocks and Lillian stopped dead in surprise. A small valley opened up before them, and there was the home of the bear people. Their houses were two and three stories high, built of logs and cedar-shingled, and set right up against the rock face of the mountain as though they had grown out of the stone. Adding a touch of whimsy were long, multicolored ribbons that hung from the corners of the roofs, fluttering like a stutter of rainbows in the breeze.

The huge man turned to look back at her. "Don't dawdle."

"It's just . . . This is so pretty."

"It's only LaOursville. Where we live."

Lillian felt somewhat heartened by the scene. Surely people who decorated their homes in such a whimsical fashion would never be prone to boiling up little girls for supper. Perhaps she really was on the verge of finding the answer to her problem.

The path down into the valley took them through more forest, which opened into thickets of berry bushes, then past an orchard twice the size of Aunt's.

A cornfield to the right and gardens to the left both had the bedraggled look of having recently been harvested. A creek came down from the mountains and ran close to the fields before it traveled away into the forest. They crossed the creek by way of a series of wide stepping-stones, and then they were on the packed dirt in front of the houses.

The man made a deep hooting sound that seemed to come from somewhere low in his chest. In response a dozen or so hairy faces peered out from various windows and doors. The only difference Lillian could see among them was that the women had shorter hair on their faces, while the men had beards as big and bushy as her companion's.

Bear people, she thought. They were big and hairy, but still people, so that was good. Surely they couldn't all be as grouchy as this one.

An older woman came slowly from one of the buildings, leaning on a staff topped with a spill of colored ribbons. Small bone carvings of bears dangled from the ends of the ribbons. Her hair had probably once been the same reddish brown as Lillian's companion's, but now it was almost completely gray. Over her raggedy clothes she wore a woven wool shawl with patterns of bears. It was edged with more bright ribbons and carvings. By contrast, the bear woman's features were stern—like Harlene in a bad mood. She stared at Lillian, then looked at the man.

"Joen," she said with a frown. "What is this you have brought?"

"Found her in the woods," Joen said. "She says Nancy Creek sent her."

The old woman spat in the dirt and Lillian's hopes drained away, along with the color in her cheeks.

"Did she say why?"

Lillian straightened her back. Maybe they *were*

going to eat her after all, but she wasn't going to stand around and let them talk about her as though she were some cow in a pasture.

"I can talk for myself, ma'am," she said.

The woman's dark gaze settled on her. "Can you now. And what do you have to say about Nancy Creek?"

"I don't know her well enough to say one thing or the other."

"Hmm. There's something about you, girl. I'm sure enough getting a queer feeling just looking at you."

"That's what your son said."

"My son?"

"Him. Joen."

"What makes you think he's my son?"

"Aren't you Mother Manan?"

"*Mother* is a title, girl."

"My name's Lillian, not *girl*."

"Well, you've got spunk, I'll give you that. Why were you sent here?"

"Aunt Nancy said you might be able to interpret a dream I had."

Mother Manan spat again at the use of Aunt Nancy's name.

"And why," she asked, "would the spider woman think we'd help *her*?"

"It's to help me, not her. And why do you call her that?" Lillian began, but then she remembered all those webs up in the rafters of Aunt Nancy's cabin, and John's joke. At least she'd *thought* it was a joke.

"Because it's in her blood," Mother Manan said. "She's from away—a place so far away that my kin have never set foot there."

"But being from somewhere else doesn't mean you're bad. Did she ever do anything to you?"

The bear woman spat again. "Her kind hunt us for our flesh and skins."

Lillian shivered. "That was long ago, ma'am," she said. "They haven't done that for years and years. And I don't think they even knew you were people when they did."

Mother Manan banged the end of her staff on the ground, jangling the bone bears in a noisy clatter.

"Maybe not," the old woman said. "But *she* knew. She was there!"

The other bear people nodded. They made an odd sound, which Lillian realized was growling, and she shivered again.

"I . . . don't know anything about that," Lillian said. "I don't even really know Aunt Nancy. I just went to her for advice."

"About a dream."

"Yes, ma'am," Lillian said.

"What kind of scheme is this?" Mother Manan demanded. "I don't interpret dreams for strangers."

"But it wasn't really her who sent me," Lillian said, correcting herself. "It was actually the spirits who sent me here."

"So now you're changing your story. How dare you try to frighten me with the notion of spirits! What kind of fool do you take me for? I've half a notion of my own to send you back to Nancy Creek as a bag of bones."

Lillian gulped. "I'm sorry to have bothered you, ma'am," she said. "I'll just go."

"Did I *say* you could go?"

"Um, no . . ."

"You didn't let me finish. Live with us for a time, look after my house. Cook and clean, and do it all without complaint. And then—when you have provided enough service in exchange for my own—*then* we will see."

"See what, ma'am?"

"If I will help you."

"I . . ."

It was like there was a wave just under the surface of everything, rolling under her feet, making everyone and everything slightly off balance. Having the dream interpreted was the only chance Lillian had to make things right again. If she went back now, Harlene would cart her off to school, and the Kindred farm would fall to ruin.

"Thank you, ma'am," she told Mother Manan. "I'll do the best I can."

"We'll see about that," the old woman said.

CHAPTER FOURTEEN

LaOursville

The first week was awful, the second week worse. Only Lillian's stubborn determination kept her at her tasks instead of flinging a broom or mop into the bear woman's face.

Mother Manan made Lillian clean the house from top to bottom, as she had no patience for even the smallest bit of dirt. Lillian worked from dawn to dusk, dusting every surface and sweeping under beds and behind dressers. Heavy cupboards had to be pulled away from the walls with no one to help. She scrubbed stone floors and walls on her knees with a bucket and brush, carrying the water back and forth from the well. She cleaned the chimney, hearth, and woodstove. She emptied and rinsed the chamber pot, a task that utterly disgusted her, but she did it without complaint.

If Mother Manan found anything Lillian had missed, she would insist that Lillian begin all over again. It was an impossible task, not helped by the endless parade of visitors who came to pay their respects to Mother Manan, none of whom bothered to wipe their feet.

Lillian also saw to Mother Manan's meals and hospitality. Paying homage to Mother Manan seemed to be the bear people's only pastime. They all had voracious appetites, so Lillian had to bake cakes and berry pies and pastries for the many visitors who came calling. She brewed tea or coffee and had to clean up everything after they were gone, only to have new guests arrive as soon as she'd finished.

When darkness fell she collapsed onto the pallet Mother Manan had provided in a small windowless room beside the pantry. She always knew when morning had come because at dawn Mother Manan would pound on the floor with her staff, summoning Lillian to another day's labor.

But she had her small rebellions.

The bear people, she discovered, hoarded food and resented sharing beyond their own clan, so she took great pleasure in throwing extra seeds to the wild birds when she was feeding Mother Manan's chickens in the nearby communal barn. After she cleaned the coop and collected the eggs, she'd milk the cows and put out saucers for the cats that lived in the barn or came soft-stepping from the forest. These cats twined around her legs and butted up against her—like the cats back on Aunt's farm once had.

Every morning she brought a biscuit and left it under what appeared to be the most gnarled and ancient tree in the orchard. "That's for you, Mr. Apple Tree Man," she'd say before returning to her endless circle of chores.

The biscuits were always gone the next day. Lillian pretended that the Apple Tree Man stepped out of his tree to eat them until the day she spied a fox darting out of the orchard with a biscuit in its mouth. That made her smile.

"You enjoy that, Mr. Fox!" she called after the thief, but the next day she put out another biscuit all the same.

The only chore that she found herself truly enjoying

came late in the afternoon, when she was sent out to the berry patches to fill a bucket. Whenever she was outside, she dawdled, taking time to talk to the birds and appreciate the beauties of the valley and LaOursville, all of which seemed so at odds with how the townsfolk lived their lives, mostly indoors with all the windows shuttered against . . . well, Lillian didn't know what. And when she went berry-picking, she went so slow that snails could have raced her to the patch and won.

~

At the beginning of her third week in LaOursville, Lillian started her day as always, making her way to Mother Manan's bedroom with a tray of biscuits smothered in honey and a steaming-hot mug of tea. She set it down on the night table and opened the heavy curtains. She stood there for a moment, still able to appreciate the beautiful view, before turning back to the foot of the bed to await Mother Manan's orders for the day.

The bear woman sat up and leaned back against the headboard. Her gaze held Lillian's, measuring and dark.

"You're doing better than I expected," she finally

said. "You work well, and without a word of complaint."

Lillian shrugged. "We made an agreement. I expect you'll soon be wanting to hear about my dream."

"Not yet. Joen tells me the barn needs cleaning. When you've finished dusting in the parlor, see to it."

What about your side of our bargain? Lillian wanted to demand, but she knew that part of the bargain was for her to work without complaint.

She left the bedroom, closing the door quietly behind her. It was all she could do to not slam it in frustration.

She'd begun to suspect that the bear people were taking out on her the bitterness they felt toward Aunt Nancy. Maybe Aunt Nancy really *had* eaten some of their kind when she was a little girl. Not like in John's story, but the way folks in the hills would shoot game for their dinner.

Because stars were stars—not holes left in some magic blanket of the night from when a bunch of spider spirits came dropping down on their silky threads to rescue a little girl. Though the bear people did appear to have a powerful fear of spiders and their webs. She'd often seen one of them shriek and jump out of the way of a spider spied on a step, or hanging from the roof of a porch.

She couldn't fathom why the spirits had told Aunt Nancy to send her here. She knew how in stories a body could be tested with all kinds of things, but this working like a slave didn't make a lick of sense.

Unless Mother Manan had never had any intention of helping her at all. Unless she was just a slave that the bear people were going to use until . . .

John's story about how the bears had planned to eat the little girl they'd put in the bottom of the well popped back into her head. Maybe they were just going to work her until she couldn't do any more. *Then* they'd probably eat her.

Maybe it was time she got herself out of this place.

~

It didn't take her long to tidy up the parlor since she'd just cleaned the whole room the day before. Taking a mop and a bucket, she filled the bucket at the well and walked down to the barn. Before she entered, she leaned on the mop and looked up into the hills surrounding LaOursville.

"I know that look."

She turned around when Joen spoke. There was that belligerent glower he always wore.

"What look is that?" she asked, hoping she didn't look as guilty as she felt.

"You're thinking of taking off into the hills."

"I'm thinking no such thing. I'm just admiring the trees and all their fancy colors."

Joen nodded. "Sure you are. But make no mistake, girl. If you run, I'll be right behind you. I'll chase you from one end of these hills to the other until I run you down. Don't think I won't."

"I'm not running anywhere," she told him. "I've got too much work to do. Wasn't it *you* who told Mother Manan that the barn needs cleaning?"

Then she picked up the bucket and mop and went into the barn. She could feel his gaze on her back, but he didn't follow. She let out a breath she hadn't been aware she was holding.

~

That afternoon while she was cleaning out the cold storage—because Mother Manan was convinced she'd seen a spider scurry under its door—Lillian found a tray of small tincture bottles. The tray was on the

top shelf and had been
pushed all the way to the
back. Lillian would never
have noticed it at all if
she hadn't been chasing
that errant spider.

The tray had clearly
been untouched and
forgotten for a very long
time. Each little bottle

had a label on it, but they were too covered in dust to read. When she blew the dust away she still couldn't read the labels because they weren't written in English. The only thing she could tell was that they all seemed to say the same thing. She felt she'd seen a bottle like this somewhere else in Mother Manan's house, but she couldn't remember where.

It wasn't until after dinner, when she was turning down Mother Manan's bed, that she remembered where she'd seen the tincture bottle. She stood with her back to the bed and looked at the long tapestry that ran from one end of the wall to the other.

It told a story, but she didn't understand what the story was.

But there was the tincture bottle. On the left side

of the tapestry, a bear, standing upright, was looking at a man dressed in what looked like Kickaha hunting leathers. In the next section he was giving the man a small brown bottle. In the last section the man stood in a meadow with his arms held out straight from his sides. Birds were sitting on his head and all along his arms, with still more fluttering around him.

Mother Manan came in while she was still looking at it.

"We don't have stories like this," Lillian said. "Not back where I'm from."

"Why would you? To your kind the animal people are only good for their fur and their meat."

Lillian didn't bother to correct her, but she knew hunting and farming weren't so black and white for everybody. And didn't the bear people keep chickens and pigs and cows?

"So what's happening in the story?" Lillian asked.

For a moment she didn't think Mother Manan would answer.

"That happened a long time ago," she finally said. "At the beginning of time, all the people could talk to each other—animals, and even people like you. But the years went by and your people forgot the old language and started hunting the animal people. There was a long war in these hills between the bears and the Kickaha that didn't end until one of my ancestors made a potion, which he gave to the medicine man you see in the tapestry. Once he tasted the potion the growls of the bear became words that he could understand. He could understand the language of every animal. That was when he finally began to respect animals and animal people. He took his knowledge back to the chiefs of his tribe, and the war came to an end."

She looked away from the tapestry to scowl at Lillian.

"But *your* people still hunt us," she said.

Lillian shook her head. "I don't. Aunt and I never hunted anything."

Mother Manan's eyes narrowed further. "Your Aunt Nancy is another matter altogether."

"She's not my aunt," Lillian said. "My aunt's name was Fran Kindred. We never hurt anybody."

"Then maybe that's why you're still alive, girl."

Lillian lay awake for a long time that night, thinking of Mother Manan's story and the tray of ancient tincture bottles she'd found in the cold storage.

CHAPTER FIFTEEN

Bottle Magic

he next morning, when Lillian was put-
ting the eggs in the cold storage, she paused in the
doorway and listened hard. She could hear Mother
Manan in the parlor with her friend Sebastian—not
what they were saying, exactly, but the steady ebb and
flow of conversation.

Stepping into the cold storage, she set the basket
of eggs on a shelf, then stood on a stool and reached
way back to the tray of tincture bottles. Were they really a magic potion that would let a body understand
the language of the animals?

She climbed down and went to the door again to listen, but the murmur of conversation continued in the parlor. She held one of the bottles to her chest and worked the stopper free. Raising it up to her nose, she gave it a sniff.

It smelled foul, but then potions almost always smelled bad. Harlene made one from some kind of fish oil that Lillian and Aunt took all the winter long. When Lillian complained about the taste, Aunt just smiled and said, "That's how you know it's working."

If she could understand the language of the animals, she could learn things without having to wait for Mother Manan to interpret her dream—that is, if she ever even intended to. That seemed more doubtful with every passing hour.

Perhaps the cats around here might know why the cats back home stared at her all the time. Maybe the chickens or pigs or cows could tell her something—like were the bear people really planning to eat her? She could track down that fox and ask why he was following her. At the very least, she might be able to make a friend or two.

But taking some of the potion was as good as stealing. Aunt hadn't raised her like that. She could well argue that she'd earned the right to take a sip of the potion with all the hard work she'd been doing. It wasn't as though anybody had told her she shouldn't give it a taste.

Oh, that? she could say, if she were asked. I had a tickle in my throat, and I thought it was some kind of cold medicine like my neighbor Harlene makes.

But who was to say it wasn't some kind of poison? Then they'd just find her lying dead here in the cold storage.

She replaced the stopper and almost put the little brown bottle back, but then she thought of Joen and the mean way he looked at her. The bear people acted like she wasn't even a person. She was just like a slave to them.

Shooting a guilty glance at the door, she pulled the stopper out again. Before she could lose her nerve, she lifted the bottle to her mouth and took a sip. She gagged on the bitter taste but managed to swallow. The awful liquid burned as it went down her throat.

Fingers shaking, she stopped the bottle again and waited.

After a few moments she decided she wasn't going to die. But she didn't feel any different, either, except she was a little sick to her stomach.

Served her right for stealing. Didn't matter how mean the bear people were.

She put the empty bottle in her pocket, then climbed back up on the stool and replaced the tray in its original spot. Putting away the eggs, she closed the door of the cold storage. She hurried to her room and hid the bottle at the bottom of her food pouch.

"Girl!" Mother Manan called from the parlor. "We'll be needing some more tea in here."

"Yes, ma'am!" she called back, and put the kettle on.

"Don't you dawdle."

"No, ma'am."

While she waited for the water to boil, she decided she didn't feel so bad after all for stealing that potion.

~

After she'd brought Mother Manan and her guest their tea and a platter of cookies, she got the wheelbarrow from the side of the house and went to the woodpile to fetch more firewood for the stove. A couple of the barn cats were sitting on the woodpile when she arrived, basking in the sun. One was a big old tom that Lillian called Rufus. He had a torn ear, and she'd seen him face off against a couple of the other cats, but he was always gentle around her. The other was a skinny black cat with a white spot in the middle of her brow. Lillian called her Star.

"Hey, Rufus," she said. "Hey, Star. Catching a little sun?"

Rufus meowed back at her the way he always did, but this time Lillian heard: "Heh. Looks like you've been sampling potions."

Lillian dropped the handles of the wheelbarrow and stared at the pair, scarcely believing her ears. "I—I can understand you," she said.

"Well, now," Rufus said, "of course you can. You must have known that would happen, elsewise you wouldn't have taken the potion. So why are you so surprised?"

"I didn't think it would really work."

"Maybe it didn't," Rufus said.

That made Star giggle.

Lillian's gaze darted from one cat to the other. "But how did you know I drank the potion?"

"That kind of thing puts a glow on a human."

Oh, no, Lillian thought. Did that mean Mother Manan would be able to tell, too? But she'd just seen her in the parlor, and she hadn't said a thing.

"Don't worry," Star said, noticing Lillian's worried look. "They're not cats. We see everything."

"I've got so much I want to ask you," Lillian started to say.

The two cats jumped down from the woodpile and ran off before she could finish.

That was just rude, Lillian thought, until she heard the footsteps coming up behind her.

"What are you doing out here?" Joen demanded.

"Getting some wood for the stove," Lillian said. "What does it look like?"

"Don't you smart-mouth me. Who were you talking to?"

Lillian sighed. "No one, sir. Well, maybe myself."

Joen studied her for a long moment with that withering gaze of his, then went on about his business. Lillian picked up the ax and split some kindling, imagining every log she hit was Joen's head.

~

She had no time to track the cats down once she finished carrying in the wood. There were other chores that needed to be done first. When they were finished, she made some bread dough and left it to rise while she went off to the berry patch. She wanted to test her new ability to understand animals, but she walked all the way to the berry patch without seeing a single one, not even a bird. There was no one around at all except for Joen, sitting on a fence way back at the edge of town, looking in her direction.

She knew why he was there. He'd taken to following her around these past few days, probably hoping she'd make a break for the woods just so he could run her down. Why did bullies enjoy being mean?

She turned her back on his distant figure and concentrated on filling her bucket.

When she was half done, she stood up to stretch her back and caught a glimpse of russet fur disappearing into the underbrush on the far side of the berry patch. She lowered her hands to her hips and looked at the spot where she'd seen the fox disappear. Foxes weren't as sly as they might think themselves to be.

Lillian crouched back down, pretending to pick more berries. "Hey, you, Mr. Fox," she called softly. "Or maybe your name's T. H. Reynolds. I know you're there. I can understand you now, so tell me, why are you following me?"

At first there was no response. Then, slowly, a long nose poked into sight, followed a moment later by the rest of the fox. He sat on his haunches in the long grass at the edge of the woods and casually licked a forepaw.

"Stay out of sight. Someone's watching me."

"Have we met?" he asked.

"Only in a dream—if you're the fox who calls himself T. H. Reynolds. Otherwise you're just a stranger who's been skulking along behind me through the mountains since I left the Creek homesteads."

"*Skulking* is rather harsh. Maybe we were just going in the same direction?"

"Except I walked along with nothing to hide, while you most certainly skulked."

"Where did we meet before?"

"You came along with me in my dream, when I was on my way to see Old Mother Possum, though you wouldn't come all the way since you ate her husband and you were afraid she'd turn you into something nasty."

"How do you know that?"

"You told me."

"Why don't I remember?"

"Because it was *my* dream, silly," Lillian said. "How

could you know? Now, if you're not going to tell me why you've been following me, you can go back into the forest and leave me be. I'm very busy."

"Hold on," the fox said. "I want to know more about this dream of yours."

"Well, you and I are the only ones who do. Mother Manan was supposed to interpret it for me—I've been working like her slave to pay for it—but she hasn't asked me one thing about it yet."

"So tell me. I'm good at figuring things out."

"I have to keep picking berries while I do it," Lillian said.

The fox nodded and started to edge out of the grass.

"Stay low," she said. "There's an eagle-eyed bear man watching me back by those buildings. Best he didn't spy you."

The fox nodded again and made his careful way to where Lillian was working. He lay in a space between the bushes while Lillian picked berries and told him her story.

"What do you think?" Lillian asked when her bucket was full and the story was done.

There was no reply. She looked to where the fox had been lying to see that he was gone. He must have slipped away through the long grass of the meadow and back into the forest.

That figured. Of course he'd go and skulk off someplace else. From the little she knew of him, that seemed to be what he did best. Except when she turned around to go back to the town she saw that Joen was halfway between the buildings and the berry patch.

The fox, she realized, was being smart, just as the cats had been earlier in the day.

Hefting her bucket onto her hip, she sashayed toward Joen and gave him a syrupy-sweet smile when she passed him by that they both knew she didn't mean. She heard him fall in silently behind her. He didn't say anything, but she could feel that suspicious gaze of his making the hairs stand up at the nape of her neck.

CHAPTER SIXTEEN

Friends

It occurred to Lillian that with winter coming on, the bear people were getting ready to hibernate. That would explain both their tendency to remain indoors and the vast quantities of food they ate.

They all seemed to be getting lazier, except for Joen. These past few days he always seemed to be someplace near to wherever Lillian was. But this morning when she went to the barn she didn't see him anywhere. That put her in such a good mood that she was humming under her breath as she stepped inside the barn.

"Oh, sing that one about the boy who liked to

crack corn," one of the cows said. "I declare, that's my favorite."

Another cow chuckled. "That's a good one, but I like the one about the ladies singing at the races."

Lillian laughed. "I'll sing them both," she said, "and anything else you want to hear."

She'd been looking forward to coming to the barn all morning. The bears might be a cranky bunch, but now she was finally making some friends.

Rufus jumped down from a rafter onto some bales of hay. He watched Lillian fetch a stool and a bucket for the milk and began to lick his lips.

"This is *my* favorite part of the day," he said.

Lillian grinned at him and began to milk the first cow, singing "Jimmy Crack Corn" and then "Camptown Races" as she'd promised. After a few more songs, she turned to Rufus.

"Yesterday Star said that cats see everything."

He looked up, his whiskers white with milk.

"It's true," he told her. "That's because we pay attention."

Lillian wanted to ask him about the cats back home—what were *they* paying attention to when they looked at her?—but the cows wanted more songs, so she sang to them while she finished milking. Then there were the chickens to see to—as gossipy a bunch as she'd ever heard—and the pigs to feed, always intent on filling their bellies.

She'd brought a honey and cheese sandwich for her breakfast and went and sat down on a bench outside the back door of the barn to eat it. The other cats had scattered after she'd given them their milk, but Rufus followed her outside.

"Do you want some?" she asked him.

"I wouldn't say no to a bit of that cheese."

But before he could take a bite he crouched down low, ears flat, gaze fixed on something that seemed to be moving toward them.

"Don't move, Lillian," he said in a soft voice. "There's danger approaching."

But saying "don't move" to Lillian was like saying "move right now." She had to turn. When she saw who it was slinking through the nearby brush, she smiled and gave a wave.

"Don't run off," she told Rufus.

"But that fox . . ."

"It's all right. It's only T.H. He's a friend of mine."

"You're friends with a *fox*?"

"You really don't have to worry. He would never eat a cat." She called over to T.H., "You don't eat cats, do you?"

T.H. trotted up to the barn.

"Not yet," he said.

Lillian frowned at him.

"Don't look at me like that," he went on. "That's just the way my friend the Russian fox says no. He says *nyet*."

Lillian pursed her lips. "Where would you meet a Russian fox?"

T.H. shrugged. "You go here and there and sooner or later you meet everyone."

He sat beside Lillian and studied Rufus. "How do, Mr. Cat," he said. "Don't believe we've had the pleasure before today."

Rufus gave the fox a suspicious look. "What does the *T.H.* stand for?" he asked.

"Truthful and Handsome. But don't go blaming me for being full of myself or anything. My mama gave me that name. Said it was something to grow into."

"You seem an unlikely pair to be friends."

T.H. nodded. "And we were an even more unlikely pair when we first met. Apparently, back then Lillian was still a kitten."

"A *kitten*?" Rufus said at the same time as Lillian said, "That was just a dream."

"Maybe yes, maybe no," T.H. said. "But I've been thinking on that. What if it wasn't a dream?"

"But it has to have been. There were magical cats and talking cows and crows and . . ."

"Foxes?" T.H. asked with a lift of one brow. "Like me? You know a lot about me from one dream."

"I don't understand that part. I just know that I can understand you today because . . . well . . ."

"You drank some magical potion."

Lillian nodded. "So you see, it's not the same at all."

"I think it's exactly the same. The cats changed a snakebit girl into a kitten, and the kitten got the possum witch to make it all as though it had never happened. It's all magic, Lillian. Doesn't matter if you go at it frontward or back."

"Is anyone going to tell me what you're talking about?" Rufus said.

"Well, now, Mr. Cat," T.H. said. "It's as simple as catching a cedar waxwing who's got himself drunk on fermented berries. You see a girl standing here, and I see a girl who used to be a kitten and who, before that, used to be a girl."

He looked at the half-eaten sandwich in Lillian's hand.

"Are you going to finish that?" he asked.

"I dreamed," Lillian told Rufus, "that I got bit by a snake and I was going to die, except these cats saved me by turning me into a kitten. But then I couldn't figure out how to be a girl again because, even if I did find some magic to make me a girl, I'd be a girl dying of a snakebite. So then I went to see Old Mother

Possum, and she . . . she turned everything back to before I got bit, and then . . ."

Lillian suddenly jumped to her feet and turned to T.H. "Do you know what this means?" she cried, then went on before he could answer. "If my dream *was* real, I can just go back to the possum witch and ask her to undo whatever it was that she did!"

"But if she'll do it—and I'm not saying she will— you'll be a kitten again."

She nodded. "That's not the point. If *I'm* the one that gets snakebit, then Aunt won't. She'll still be alive! I'd rather be a kitten forever if it means Aunt doesn't have to die."

"Are you saying *this* is all a dream?" Rufus asked. "Because it doesn't feel like it to me."

"Me, either," T.H. said. "Interesting, isn't it?"

"No," the cat said. "It's confusing. And more than just a little disturbing."

"That's it," Lillian said. "I'm going back to Black Pine Hollow and Old Mother Possum. Now."

"Hold on there," T.H. said. "What's the hurry? If you run off now, those bears will chase you down before you get as far as the berry patch."

"Aunt doesn't have to be dead," Lillian said. "Don't you understand? All those horrible things don't have to have happened."

"Yes, yes," T.H. said. "That's clear. But really, I've got to ask you again, what's the hurry? However long it takes to get to Black Pine Hollow won't matter. If you do manage to convince the possum witch to help you turn the clock back a second time—whether it's today or a week from today—it will still be like no time has passed for anyone."

"It'll have passed for me," Lillian said. "But if it makes you feel any better, I'll wait until they're all asleep before I sneak out."

T.H. nodded. "That makes sense. Do you want some company on your journey?"

"You mean with you walking at my side instead of skulking around in the underbrush nearby?"

"You need to let that go. I didn't know who you were then."

"But you were still following me."

He gave another nod. "Because I was curious. I saw all the cats watching you, and I felt some connection to you, but I didn't know what it was. Now I do."

Lillian was so giddy with the thought that she might truly be able to make it so that Aunt had never died that she decided to stop teasing him.

"I'd be happy for the company," she said.

"Now about that other half of your sandwich," T.H. said.

Lillian laughed and laid it on the bench. "Be my guest."

"I'll wait for you in the woods," T.H. said, munching happily. "Where the path starts."

Lillian nodded. "I'll see you tonight."

CHAPTER SEVENTEEN

The Big Black Spider

It was hard, hard, hard to go through the rest of the day pretending that nothing had happened and she wasn't going to run away tonight. But it had, and she was.

It seemed impossible that the possum witch had been able to turn back time. But it made sense. It was why both she and Aunt Nancy felt there was something unbalanced with the world—and it did have everything to do with her. It explained why the cats had been staring at her. They'd known the problem all along. They just hadn't been able to tell her.

But she knew now, and she was the only one who could fix things—so long as Old Mother Possum would help her. So long as she *could*.

Lillian didn't know much about magic. Maybe a witch couldn't do the same spell twice in a row. But there *had* to be a way to make things right again. She'd do whatever it took to bring Aunt back. She'd live her whole life as a kitten. She'd even die as a snakebit girl.

~

Later that afternoon she went out to the well for water. On the way back, skinny Star came up beside her and followed her up onto the side porch that led into the kitchen. Lillian glanced around to make sure no one was looking.

"Hey, Star," she said in a soft voice. "How're you doing?"

She patted the cat and it arched its back, purring, before it backed away.

"You need to stop that," she said. "I can't think straight when you're petting me, and I've got a message for you."

"What kind of a message? Is it from T.H.?"

"Like I'd be delivering messages for a fox."

"Sorry. Who's it from?"

"Rufus says if you're going to go, you've got to go *now*. The bears think you've been spying for the spider woman, but they weren't sure. Now Joen says he's got proof."

"I'm not spying for anybody."

"That's as may be, but it doesn't change anything."

"What kind of proof would he have?"

"I don't know," Star said, "but he's got a bottle in his pocket that he's guarding real careful."

Lillian's heart sank. "You mean like a little brown bottle for tinctures?"

"No, it's bigger than that, and the glass is clear. But that's all I could see. I don't know what's in it."

It was the wrong time, but Lillian knew she had to run now. Except just then the kitchen door opened. Star darted away and Lillian was left alone to face Mother Manan.

"What are you doing out here, girl?"

"I was just getting some water and petting the cat."

"I don't remember petting cats being part of your chores."

"No, ma'am. Ah—was there something you wanted?"

The bear woman nodded. "I need you in the parlor."

Lillian considered bolting, right there and then, but she knew how fast Joen was, and Mother Manan would have him on her tail as quick as you could shake a stick. The whole plan was to *sneak* off so that no one would know she was gone until morning and she was miles and miles away.

Sighing, she picked up the bucket and followed Mother Manan into the kitchen. She left the bucket there and continued on to the parlor with the old woman.

Of course Joen had to be in there, too.

"What did you want, ma'am?" Lillian asked.

Mother Manan lowered herself into her chair. Joen's eyes were still mean, but his mouth had pulled into a satisfied smirk. It didn't look any more pleasant than his usual scowl.

"Joen found something in your room," Mother Manan said, nodding to Joen, who pulled a jar out from behind his back.

Lillian couldn't see what was inside because of his big fingers. But then he put it down on the table. There was a big black spider inside—the kind you could sometimes find on logs down by the creek be-

low Aunt's farm, or in the outhouse, with a body the size of a man's thumb and fat, hairy legs.

"I've never seen that jar before," Lillian said truthfully.

"And the spider?"

Lillian picked the jar up and noticed how Mother Manan gave a little shiver when she did. Even Joen looked—well, not exactly frightened, but wary.

Lillian peered inside the jar at the poor trapped spider.

"I can't tell one from the other," she said. "Besides, there's spiders everywhere."

"Not in LaOursville. We've managed to keep them scarce here."

Lillian shook her head. "Well, I didn't bring it in. Why are you so upset about spiders, anyways? They eat bugs and such, not people. Or bears."

"And yet," Mother Manan said, "when the spider woman was a little girl—about the age you are now—she ate my great-great-great-grandpappy."

"That's just a story. And even if it were true, it happened too long ago for Aunt Nancy to have been that little girl. She'd have to be ancient."

But as she spoke, Lillian remembered the Creek boys' story. John had been joking when he said that Aunt Nancy was that little girl—hadn't he? And didn't they say back home that Aunt Nancy had been living on the rez for centuries?

"You yourself told us the spider woman sent you," Mother Manan said. "And we want to know why."

"I told you the why. She said that the spirits told her that you might be able to interpret my dream. It sure wasn't to bring spiders into your house. Whyever would she do that? Even if what you're saying is true, it all happened too long ago for anybody to care about it now."

"We don't forget," Mother Manan said with a low growl. "And neither does she."

Lillian sighed. Of course they didn't. If there was one thing these hills could breed, it was a feud that went on long after anybody should remember what started it.

"Well, I'm not part of your stupid feud," Lillian said. She stood up, still holding the jar. "Now pardon me," she said, "but I need to get my blanket and stuff."

She didn't think they'd actually let her just walk off, but she figured it was worth a shot. Like Aunt always said, you don't get anything without trying for it first.

"You're leaving?" Mother Manan said. "What about your dream?"

"I don't need you to figure it out for me—not that I believe you were ever going to keep your side of the bargain. Shame on you. Looks like you need to find yourself a new slave."

"You watch your manners!" Joen told her.

Lillian simply turned away. The hair prickled at the nape of her neck again, but nobody came after her as she went to gather her blanket, canteen, and food pouch.

"What that girl needs is a good licking," she heard Joen say in the other room.

"And if she calls the spiders down on us?" Mother Manan retorted. "You have any idea how many are living in the woods around us? Probably thousands."

"So we lock her up. I have ways to make her tell us why the spider woman sent her here."

Lillian slipped into the kitchen and put bread, cheese, and apples in her pouch. She thought she'd free the poor spider as soon as she got out the door, so she picked up the jar once more. Just as she was about to leave, she came smack up on Joen, blocking her way. He looked smug, hands on his hips.

"Just where do you think you're going, little missy?" he said.

"A place you've never heard of. It's called Mind Your Own Business."

He glared at her, lines furrowing his brow. "I'll teach you a thing or two about how to talk to—"

"That will be quite enough, Joen," Mother Manan said from behind him.

His glare held for a moment longer, and then he ducked his head down and stepped out of Mother Manan's way.

"Yes, ma'am," he said.

Lillian had to hide a giggle at how easily the big tough bear man was chastened by the old woman.

Mother Manan moved closer.

"Saying you're not in the spider woman's employ," she said, "what's made you turn against us today?"

For a long moment Lillian could only stare at her, too surprised to speak. Then she shrugged. "There's really no point in talking about it. None of this matters anymore." She tried to pass the bear woman, but Mother Manan blocked Lillian with her staff.

"Tell me why, at least," the old woman said, "you were willing to work all this time in the hope that I would interpret your dream, but suddenly you have no more interest in what it means. Unless, of course, someone else interpreted it for you."

Lillian shook her head. "No, I worked it out for myself."

"I see. So what did it tell you?"

"Nothing that would mean anything to anyone except me."

The old woman bristled. "My patience isn't endless, girl. Tell me now, or we'll see how a few days locked in a dark cellar will loosen your tongue."

"All right," Lillian said.

Except what she did instead was kick the bucket of water across the floor, pop the lid off the jar she was still holding, and toss the big spider at them. They screeched and jumped to either side as Lillian darted between them. Joen made a grab for her, but he slipped in the water and crashed down hard. She leaped right over his reaching arm and sped out the door and across the packed dirt in front of the houses.

CHAPTER EIGHTEEN

Escape!

The bear man came after Lillian, but she had a head start. Despite his size, he was obviously hurting from the fall and slower than the fleet-footed girl who'd run hundreds of races with the Welches' dogs, spent months learning how to repair a farm, and worked so hard for Mother Manan that her strength and stamina were at their peak.

His legs were longer, but she was more agile. For every two steps the bear man took, she took three, and slowly but surely she drew farther ahead of him. The forest grew near, but Joen was still close behind her.

She couldn't keep this speed up forever. Maybe Joen
could. And then he'd catch up and drag her back to
LaOursville.

"Help, help!" she cried out, hoping T.H. might
hear her.

She didn't know if he was around. It was so much
earlier than they'd planned for her escape. And she
didn't think the fox could do much if it came to a
fight with the bear man. She glanced back. Joen was
still coming. Was he closer?

She sped up. Pain stitched her side as she pushed
herself to keep running. She was past the berry
bushes now and under the first few outlying trees.

Ahead of her, the path cut through the cliff. Another glance back showed Joen still in pursuit.

"Help!" she called again.

She was surprised when she got an answer from a completely unexpected quarter. A strange thrumming sound made her glance back again to see a cloud of birds descending on the bear man. Mostly small ones—robins and sparrows and wrens—but there were even a few crows and jays in the unruly flock. Joen had to slow down, batting his hands around his head.

Lillian ducked under a branch that she was about to run into. She steered herself back onto the path and turned to look once more as she heard an unholy screeching.

Along with the birds, cats of every shape and color had come out of the grass and were launching themselves at the bear man. Joen stumbled to a halt. He dropped to his knees, pulling cats off. But for every one he pulled off, two more were scratching and clawing at him while the birds buffeted his face and pecked at his nose.

Lillian stopped to look at the astonishing sight. She leaned against a tree, gasping for air. What had gotten into the birds and cats? They didn't even all get along in the first place. So why had they suddenly joined forces to attack Joen?

Then she remembered all those weeks of putting out saucers of milk for the cats and throwing extra feed to the wild birds. Perhaps this was their way of saying thank you kindly.

Lillian grinned. Maybe the cows would be coming along next, or an apple tree man was stirring in his woody home, getting ready to give Joen a good bang on the head.

"What are you waiting for?" a familiar voice asked.

She turned to see T.H. stepping out of the under-brush.

"Where were you?" she asked.

"On my way to finding out why you needed help."

"I'm okay now," she said. Then she motioned with her chin to where Joen was still trying to fend off her rescuers. "Have you ever seen such a thing?" she added.

"No. And if you ever want to see *anything* again, you'd be smart to keep moving. Cats and birds can't hold a bear man forever. We'll want a good head start before he comes tracking us through the forest."

He was right. Lillian pushed herself away from the tree.

"Thank you, thank you!" she called back to her rescuers.

She set off at a jog up the trail, T.H. trotting at her side. They slipped through the cleft in the rocks and then they were in the forest proper, tall trees rearing up all around the path.

"Why was the big lug chasing you?" he asked after they'd put some distance behind them.

"I had to run away before they locked me up in a cellar. They found a spider in my room and said I was a spy for the spider woman, which is what they call Aunt Nancy up on the rez. And Mother Manan was mad that I wouldn't tell her about my dream, or what it meant."

She glanced back down the path. There was still no sign of Joen.

"Do you really think he'll follow me?" she asked.

"Depends how mad you made him."

"Really mad."

"Then I think he'll track us for as long as it takes to find us, and he'll probably have a gang of his friends in tow."

Lillian knew T.H. was right. Joen had been set on bullying her, and he was too stubborn to give up. He'd do whatever it took to bring her back, holding to his task like a hillside of kudzu, as Aunt would say.

But Lillian was more determined than she'd ever been to make things right again. She needed to get back to Old Mother Possum.

"How can we lose him?" she asked.

"Oh, I know a trick or two about avoiding folks dogging my trail," T.H. said. "The big question is, will he be tracking us with his nose or his eyes?"

"I don't understand."

"Will he be a bear or a man?" T.H. clarified.

Lillian tensed. Bad enough to have that big man

chasing after them, but if he could also be a bear . . .
well, she didn't know how they'd get away from him.

"How good are you at climbing trees?" the fox
asked her.

"The first time we met I was up in a tree, but I don't
suppose you'd remember that."

"Nope. Now let's put some miles behind us."

"Why did you want to know if I can climb?"

"Man or bear, he's going to be looking for sign or
following your scent on the trail," the fox said, "But
if you take to the trees like a squirrel and stay up there,
he's not going to find either. We just need to find the
right place."

~

Before long, T.H. found what he was looking for.
He had Lillian wade into the stream that ran alongside the path until she came to a large, low-hanging
bough. With the stones slippery underfoot, it took
her a couple of tries to jump up and get enough grip
on the branch to pull herself out of the water. The
bough dipped under her weight, almost putting her
back in the stream, but she was able to hoist herself
around and scramble up its length.

"The wind's from the east," the fox called up to her. He pointed his long nose toward the west. "So go that way."

The trees grew close to each other here, their branches overlapping, making it easy for Lillian to move from one to the other. T.H. called for her to stop when she was a good distance west of the stream.

"What now?" she asked.

"Now you find yourself a comfortable crook in that tree, and we wait."

"What about you?"

"I'll keep out of sight. He's not looking for a fox."

Lillian climbed a little higher, to where a fat branch split off from the main trunk. Once she'd settled in with her back to the trunk, she found she could still see a small stretch of the trail through the branches. Below her perch she could just make out T.H. lying amid a stand of tall ferns.

"I can see a bit of the trail from here," she called down to him. "Doesn't that mean Joen might see me?"

"Only if he's looking up. Now shush. We can't be talking, or the noise of our yapping will make all this hiding pointless."

"But I don't see why—"

"Shush!"

Lillian sighed. What seemed pointless was hiding, and the longer they did it, the more pointless it seemed. They should be putting as much distance between themselves and LaOursville as they could, because the sooner they got to Black Pine Hollow, the sooner all of this would get fixed. Yes, she'd be a cat again, but Aunt would be alive.

Aunt would be *alive*.

She was about to call down to T.H. again when a barn swallow flew by her tree, crying, "They're coming, they're coming!"

The swallow wasn't alone. She could see other small birds flying about the forest, passing along the same message. The barn swallow made an abrupt turn in the air and came back to Lillian's tree, where it landed on a branch just a foot or so from her face.

"There you are!" it cried in its high, piping voice. "Be careful, be ever so careful. The bears are coming!"

"The bears? What do you mean, *bears*?"

But the swallow had already flown off. It didn't matter. Lillian knew exactly what it meant: Joen had brought some of the others to help him.

"Will you shush up there!" T.H. called in a hoarse whisper.

"I know, but . . ."

Her voice trailed off. She pressed herself into the bark of her tree, wishing she could disappear, because there they were. Big brown shapes loped along the forest path, moving quickly and silently for all their bulk. She caught only fleeting glimpses of them through the thick network of branches, but that was enough to show her that they weren't bear people from LaOursville. They were bears. *Real bears. Foot bears.*

Though they were out of sight now, she held her breath, waiting, straining to hear. What were they doing? Had they guessed the trick that had been played on them? Were they sneaking toward her right now?

She supposed that they'd reached the spot where she'd stepped into the stream, because suddenly she could hear their quarreling voices.

What were those bears arguing about? She could *almost* make out the words. . . .

Leaning away from the tree to try to hear better, she slipped and scrabbled at the bark with her fingers until she regained her balance. She waited, biting her lip, to see if she'd been heard.

There were fewer voices now, and when she looked in the direction of the path she saw a brown shape go by, heading back in the direction of LaOursville. A moment later it was followed by another, then more, all of them only briefly glimpsed as they moved along the limited view she had of the trail.

She had no idea if they'd all gone back or not. Maybe some had stayed. Joen would have stayed.

It seemed to take forever before T.H. finally returned. He looked up with a grin.

"It worked," he said. "They've gone back to their valley."

"All of them?"

"Each and every."

"What were they arguing about?"

The fox shrugged. "Just over Joen's insisting that they keep trying to find your trail."

"But he's gone, too?"

"Yes. Joen's got quite a limp on him, but I saw the look in his eyes. He'll be back."

"So we should go as quick as we can now." She started to come down the tree.

"Hold on," T.H. said. "Before you come down, why don't you see how far you can go squirrel-style?

The branches seem pretty close still, and the farther you can go before you put your scent back on the ground, the better it will be."

"I guess I could do that."

The fox nodded. "I'll scout ahead. I'm sure there's got to be another trail over on the far side of the mountain. If we're lucky, the bears won't know anything about it, or maybe they won't go looking for us there."

"You go ahead and find that trail," she said. "I'll follow along as best I can."

T.H. slipped away. At first she could see the plume of his tail poking up through the underbrush, but then branches got in the way and he was lost to sight. Lillian gave a last look back to the trail, hoping there wasn't a bear sneaking along after them. She edged her way along the branch until she could grab a limb of the next tree over and swing herself into its canopy. She repeated the maneuver from tree to tree and, while she wasn't nearly as fast as a squirrel, she made progress at her own slow pace.

Eventually she ran out of branches growing close enough to each other. It was time to come down, anyway. The last light of the setting sun disappeared just as she made her way to the ground.

She wanted to call for T.H., except
that might bring Joen to her rather
than the fox, so she sat down on the roots of the big
tree and waited for him to return.

Although Lillian was expecting him, she jumped
when T.H. suddenly appeared out of the brush.

T.H. grinned. "Good job. You came much farther
than I expected. It'll take the bears forever to pick up
your scent all this way from where they lost it."

They shared some of the food Lillian had taken
from Mother Manan's kitchen. Lillian would have
liked to go on, but there was no moon, and the pale

starlight couldn't make its way down through the thick canopy. She didn't have T.H.'s night sight, and it was too dark for her to see. So she sat against the tree trunk, cozy in her blanket, T.H. curled up at her side.

"What do you think?" Lillian asked dreamily. "Could that story the Creek boys told me be true?"

"It's a good story."

"But is it true? Are those stars really the holes left behind by spiders who dropped down to rescue their kin? Or are they just specks of light up in the night sky?"

"Why can't they be both?"

"What's that supposed to mean?"

"Well, when you were a kitten, you were also a girl, weren't you?"

"I suppose."

Lillian sat for a while, listening to T.H.'s breathing start to even out.

"I have a bone to pick with Aunt Nancy," she grumbled before he was completely asleep.

T.H. sighed. "Why's that?"

"Why? Because she sent me on a wild-goose chase."

"But if she hadn't sent you to the bear people, you'd never have gotten the potion from Mother Manan, and we wouldn't have been able to talk to each other and figure it all out the way we did."

"Aunt Nancy wouldn't have known anything about that potion."

"But maybe the spirits who told her to send you to the bear people did."

Lillian frowned. "I don't know. I wish people would just say what they really mean instead of getting all tricksy about it. Both Aunt Nancy and Mother Manan tricked me. It wasn't any fun being a slave."

"Just think of it as something that builds character."

"I've got plenty of character."

The fox chuckled. "That you do."

CHAPTER NINETEEN

Back to Black Pine Hollow

illian woke just before dawn from a nightmare in which the bears had captured her and were about to cook her up in a big pot in Mother Manan's kitchen. She'd tangled herself in her blanket. Wrenching her arms free, she sat up to find T.H. sitting on his haunches a few feet away. He studied her with a curious gaze.

"You're a restless sleeper," he said.

"I had a bad dream. The bears were cooking me up for supper."

"I'd be surprised if that hasn't made you lose your appetite."

Lillian smiled. "Are you offering to have my share of breakfast?"

"It's what a friend would do."

"Maybe, but I'm hungry, so I don't think so."

The sun began to rise while they were eating. By the time they were finished, the morning twilight had given way to the sun, so they started back across the mountains.

Eventually they passed the tree where the hunter had been hidden.

"I wonder if he ever got that panther," Lillian said.

"I doubt that. They're wily—almost as wily as foxes."

"And probably not as humble."

"Probably not," T.H. agreed.

T.H. told stories along the way, and Lillian taught him some of the songs that she'd learned from Aunt. After the horrible weeks Lillian had spent in LaOursville, the day felt like a special outing.

The time passed quickly, and the distance with it, since much of the trail was downhill. By late afternoon they were back in the familiar hills around Aunt's farm. They tromped through the marsh to just within sight of the big pine tree that marked the possum witch's home.

"This is as far as I go," T.H. said.

"I know. Because you ate her husband."

He gave her a sour look. "He was already dead."

"So you said."

"Well, he *was*. Truthful and Handsome, remember?"

Lillian nodded. She stood there looking at the dead pine. Even though she'd already met Old Mother Possum, or maybe just dreamed they'd met it was all a bit confusing—she was still nervous.

"I wonder what will happen," she said. "What if I'm wrong? What if she can't help me? What if it *was* just a dream?"

"I don't know," T.H. said. "I just know there's only one way to find out."

Lillian nodded. Shouldering her blanket and pack, she picked her way through the soggy marsh to where the tall dead pine rose from a small hillock ahead of her. As twilight turned into night she could see all the little medicine and tincture bottles tied to the branches of the pine. When she reached the hillock the ground firmed under her feet.

She stood for a moment, remembering the last time she'd been here. It couldn't have been a dream. How could she remember it all so clearly?

She cleared her throat, then called into the deepening shadows that surrounded the pine.

"Hello hello? Are you there, Mrs. Possum?"

The tincture bottles clanged lightly in a discordant song as Lillian waited for an endless moment.

The figure that finally stepped quietly out of the tree's shadows was just as she recalled. Old Mother Possum was still some strange combination of woman and possum, but whereas before she'd towered over the kitten Lillian had been, now she was a good head and a half shorter.

She leaned on a staff that reminded Lillian of Mother Manan's. Braided strips of leather encased the top, then longer strands with tiny bottles tied to their ends swung freely. The bottles on the staff echoed the song of the tree, and the possum witch's small black eyes studied Lillian intensely.

"This is interesting," she said. "I don't get many human visitors, and never one so young as you. Have you come for a potion, girl? Something to make some boy love you? Or maybe you're looking for wealth or power—a piece of magic that can take you out of these hollows and into the wide world beyond?"

Lillian shook her head. "I'm the kitten you met at the beginning of the summer."

"I see. And the reason we met was?"

"I was a kitten. You turned me back into a girl."

"That seems unlikely. I can't stop the tales they tell of me, but the truth is I don't have the kind of mojo something like that would take. And if I did find a way to do it, I'm fairly certain I'd remember it."

Lillian shook her head. "I'm not saying this right. You didn't so much change me from a kitten to a girl as send me back in time so that it didn't happen in the first place—my being changed from a girl into a kitten, I mean. By the cats."

"You'd think I'd remember that as well."

"Well, it's true."

But even as she spoke the words Lillian realized that she hadn't thought this through. When she'd gone back to that time before the snake bit her, not only had she not been bitten by the snake anymore, but so far as Old Mother Possum was concerned, Lillian had never met *her* before, either.

Old Mother Possum nodded. "I can see that you

believe what you're telling me, but it's not so clear for me."

She studied Lillian again for so long that Lillian began to fidget. Old Mother Possum tapped her staff lightly on the ground and the bottles sang once more. The old woman listened intently, then appeared to come to a decision.

"My bottles sense some familiarity about you, otherwise I'd send you on your way. Come inside," she said, "Let's see if we can get to the bottom of this."

Lillian gave the tree a dubious look. She didn't see anything that looked like a window, never mind a door.

"You didn't come inside the last time?" Old Mother Possum asked.

Lillian shook her head. She wasn't one bit sure about this, but at least the possum witch was starting to believe her.

Old Mother Possum motioned toward the dead pine. "The trick," she said, "is to simply walk forward and expect there to be a door to let you in."

"Really?"

"Just do what I do."

Lillian watched as the old woman walked forward.

Just when she was about to walk smack into the tree, she vanished.

Lillian stared at the tree. She didn't think she could do that. But then she thought of Aunt, remembered her still, gray features the last time she'd seen her, lying in her coffin before they nailed the lid on. Straightening her shoulders, she took a breath and walked toward the tree.

There's a door, there's a door, there's a door. . . .

She flinched as she was about to walk into the tree, but then the tree wasn't there and she stumbled forward. A bony hand caught her and helped her regain her balance. She blinked in the light, though it wasn't bright, then looked around in wonder.

Where there should have been, at most, a hollow tree, was instead the interior of a cozy cottage with a stone floor and wooden walls. A small fire burned in a hearth with two chairs in front of it and a carpet under the chairs. There were candles on the mantel, and more on the wooden table in the center of the room. She spied a small bed in a corner with a chest at its foot. On the opposite wall, a cluttered counter ran the length of the room, filled with all kinds of

little jars and boxes and bottles. Drying herbs hung from the rafters above.

Lillian looked up. Why would there be rafters inside a tree? How could any of this even be real?

She turned back to where she'd come in. Framed by the doorway, she could still see the marsh out there.

"Is—is this magic?" she asked.

Her hostess smiled. "No, it's simply my home."

The old woman led Lillian to one of the chairs by the fire. "I was about to pour myself some tea when you came calling," she said. "Would you like some?"

"Yes, please."

Old Mother Possum fussed with a teapot, cups, saucers, and honey at the long counter. Taking some biscuits out of a small crock, she set them on a flowered plate.

"Would you mind?" she said, holding the plate out to Lillian.

Lillian got up and carried the plate over to a small table between their chairs. The biscuits smelled just like Aunt's—heavenly.

The possum woman handed Lillian a cup of tea, then returned for her own. Picking up a small handloom, she made her way back to her own chair.

She took a sip of her tea and a bite of biscuit and smacked her lips in appreciation before setting both back on the saucer.

"Now, let's see," she said, holding the loom on her lap.

She bent down to examine the unfinished tapestry, and Lillian leaned closer to look at it as well. It appeared to be an endless flurry of leaves, eddying in a breeze so that they floated one over the other.

Lillian didn't know much about weaving, but she didn't need to in order to know that the workmanship was exquisite. Color and shading gave the leaves the appearance of having fallen onto the cloth, rather than being woven into it.

Old Mother Possum sifted through the loose wool that hung from the end of the loom, her thin fingers deftly separating one strand from the other until she finally pulled one free.

"Here we are," she said.

"What is it?"

"Let's see. A night early in the summer. A kitten in the marsh, spraying mud and water onto my bottles to make them sing. And then . . . ah, yes . . ."

"I don't see anything," Lillian said around a mouthful of biscuit. "What are you looking at?"

"Possibilities. All the things that *could* happen, depending on the choices we make."

Her gaze lifted to capture Lillian's.

"Things didn't turn out so happily for you, did they?" the possum woman said.

Lillian shook her head. "Can you fix it?"

"By *fix it*, do you mean return things to when you were still a kitten asking for my help?"

242

"Please."

"Of course I can."

Lillian waited eagerly, but the old woman merely set the loom aside and picked up her tea once more.

"Um," Lillian finally began.

"I'll be needing some kind of payment," Old Mother Possum said.

Stupid, stupid, Lillian thought. She was so stupid. Of course the possum witch would want some kind of payment.

"I don't have anything," she said. "Last time   "

Old Mother Possum's eyebrows rose.

"Last time?" she prompted when Lillian didn't go on.

"Last time you didn't ask for anything."

"Goodness. I must have been feeling generous that night."

But then Lillian remembered the tincture bottle at the bottom of her food pouch. Pulling it out, she gave it to the possum witch.

"I have this," she said.

Old Mother Possum smiled as she held the bottle up to the light.

"This will make a nice addition to my tree," she

said, "but it's such a small thing to trade for a big magic. Do you have anything else?"

"Maybe I could do something for you in trade?" Lillian tried.

The possum witch nodded. "Now, that's a fine idea. Why don't you tell me your story?"

"My story?"

"A story a body's never heard before can be just as good as coin. Better, if it's a good one."

"But didn't your loom tell you everything that happened?" Lillian asked.

"Stories are meant to be told," Old Mother Possum responded, settling herself in her chair.

"I'm in kind of a hurry."

Old Mother Possum smiled. "There's no rush, dear. Whether I return you at this moment or in an hour, you'll still go back to the exact same point in time. It's just the way it works."

Lillian fidgeted impatiently in her chair and turned her teacup around and around on its saucer. "But Aunt—"

"Will still be there. You'll still be a kitten. Everything will be the way it was. So we have time for your story."

"It's not very interesting."

"Really?"

"Well, big chunks of it aren't."

"So tell me the parts that are," Old Mother Possum said. "Unless you have something else to trade?"

"Well, the worst part," Lillian began, "was when I got back to the farm and found Aunt lying in the corn patch. . . ."

~

Lillian had almost finished a second mug of tea before she came to the end of her story. She'd skimmed over some parts, and she hadn't said why T.H. had stayed behind both times she'd come to Black Pine Hollow.

"So he's out there in the marsh right now?" Old Mother Possum asked when Lillian was finished.

Lillian nodded slowly.

"Now, I've never known a shy fox. Nor one to pass up the chance for a free meal."

"Oh, he's just . . . um . . . you know . . ."

"In fact, I do. He thinks I'm mad at him for eating my husband."

"You knew all along? And you're not mad?"

"Why would I be? William was already dead. It's the natural order of things, whether we go back into the earth or fill somebody's stomach."

"How did you know?"

Old Mother Possum smiled. "You do remember I'm a witch, don't you? What you and your friend might have asked was, how could I *not* know?"

"I suppose. Well, T.H. will be happy to hear that."

That made the possum woman laugh.

"Oh, he won't believe you," she said. "He'll just think it's some trick to get him to drop his guard so that I can catch him in a spell."

"Why would he think that?"

"Because it's how a fox's mind works. He's always sly himself, so naturally he expects the same of others."

"I wouldn't play a trick on him."

"And maybe he even believes it," Old Mother Possum said, then she stood up. "Well, this has been very nice, but it's time you went back and the world gets itself all rearranged once more."

"Will—will it hurt?"

"Did it hurt the last time?"

"No."

"Then why should this be any different?" the possum witch asked.

Before Lillian could reply, Old Mother Possum snapped her fingers—

CHAPTER TWENTY

The Girl Who Was a Kitten Again

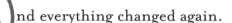

nd everything changed again.

One moment she was a girl, sitting in a chair by a fire, the next she was a kitten, standing outside in the marsh with the tall dead pine rearing up above her. The only thing that didn't change was that Old Mother Possum was present in both places. But whereas a moment ago Lillian had looked down at the woman from her taller height, now she was looking up because she was a kitten again.

"Is—is everything back to normal?" she asked.

"Oh, nothing ever changed here," the possum

witch told her. "I just let you have a look-see at one of the other paths that run alongside this world of ours. Other possibilities, if you will."

Lillian looked at her, confusion plain in her kitten eyes.

"My bottles catch and hold the winds," Old Mother Possum explained. "Not just from this world, but from all worlds—ones that were, ones that might could be. I wanted you to see that small choices can have large consequences.

So I had the bottles sing a song that opened a portal to one of those other possibilities. You ran through that portal thinking of yourself as a little girl, so that was the shape you wore on that particular journey. But as I say, it was merely one of many possibilities."

"Do you mean it wasn't *real*? That I was still a kitten here the whole time I thought I was a girl again?"

The possum witch nodded. "Nothing changed here while you were gone. The only place something might have been changed for you is in here." She laid a palm on her chest. "In your heart. In how you see the world."

"So it was . . . some kind of lesson?"

She supposed she had learned a thing or two. She now knew something about looking after a farm, and standing up for herself, and how true friends will stand by you, and the senselessness of holding on to old quarrels. She'd even learned that sometimes a thing was just going to happen—like if one person weren't bitten by a snake, then maybe somebody else would be.

Old Mother Possum shrugged. "What's important to remember is that one thing leads to another. Trouble is, it's hard to see ahead sometimes, so I gave you a chance to do just that."

"You didn't turn back time?"

"I know it's hard to understand, but there are possibilities and consequences with every choice you make. For now, just think of it like a dream, where a lot of things happened, but you were only asleep for a moment."

"But—"

"I'm not God, kitten. I can't turn back time."

"Is there really a whole cottage inside that dead tree?" Lillian asked.

"What do you think?"

"I don't know how it can be, but I think there is."

Old Mother Possum tapped a bottle tied to a nearby branch. It clinked against another.

"There *is* magic," she said.

Lillian nodded. "But you don't have enough magic to change me back into a girl?" she asked.

"I'm afraid not."

"And if I do find someone to help me . . . does that mean the dream I had about Aunt dying and everything . . . will that come true?"

"That was another road from the one you're on now, kitten. Nobody can tell where this one will take you."

Lillian nodded. "Thank you," she said. "I won't forget what you've shown me."

"Don't make a promise you can't keep," the possum witch said.

"What do you mean?"

"Folks in your situation . . . Well, let's just say it doesn't tend to stick. The farther away you get from marvels, the harder it is to remember them. I've seen it happen a hundred times before."

Lillian shook her head. "I could *never* forget all of this. I don't want to forget any of it."

"That's as may be, but I will still give you the gift of memory, so that one day you will remember it all again. I can't say when it will happen, but happen it will."

Lillian didn't bother to argue. She knew how impossible it would be to forget.

Old Mother Possum bent down and gave her a pat.

"Run along now," she said. "And be careful. A kitten can seem a tasty snack to a hungry predator."

"I'll be careful. But I won't give up trying to find a way to change back."

The old woman nodded. "I understand. But consider—it might seem like a terrible thing to be trapped in a kitten's body, but there are worse fates."

Then she stepped back into the tree and was gone.

Lillian stared at the bottle tree for a long moment. Old Mother Possum was right about that. She'd already seen one of those worse fates.

She made her way back to where she'd left T.H., being careful not to set the bottles clinking against one another. Her paws got wet and mud-caked again, but she didn't care. She was trapped as a kitten, but she didn't care about that, either. Aunt was alive. That was all that mattered.

As she came to the tree line, T.H. rose up from the ferns where he'd been lying, startling her.

"So she wasn't able to help?" he asked.

"What do you mean? She changed everything back."

"Back to what? You still look like a kitten to me."

"But—"

Except then Lillian realized that, so far as T.H. was concerned, the kitten she was again had simply wandered down to the pine, had a conversation with the possum witch, and then come back. He knew nothing of the months she'd spent as a girl, mourning the loss of Aunt, the journey to LaOursville, their escape, or anything.

"I know it seems like not much happened," she said,

"but the little while you've been waiting here has been months for me, and for you, too."

"Ha, ha."

"No, it's true."

"How can it be true?" he asked.

So as they walked away from Black Pine Hollow, the kitten following the trail the fox took so that she didn't fall into the water, Lillian told him all the things that had happened from when she found herself back in the body of the little girl again.

"That's impossible," he said when she was done.

"I was a girl, and now I'm a kitten," Lillian said. "I can talk to animals and birds. I was supposed to die from the snakebite but I didn't. That should all be impossible, too."

"If any of that happened."

"You don't believe me?"

"I don't know what to think. The only reason your story makes any sense is that you don't act like the same little kitten I met earlier tonight. Sometime between your seeing the witch and coming back, you've changed. You seem older. You don't even talk exactly the same."

"I learned some important things, but I'm still Lillian the girl, even though I'm a cat, too."

The fox shrugged. "I don't understand how you can be both a girl and a cat."

"Here," Lillian said, stopping at a pool of water. "Look at this."

T.H. looked over her shoulder to see the reflection of a redheaded girl where there should have been one of a calico kitten.

"Well, I'll be," he said.

"Now do you believe me?"

"I have to, don't I? But I'm still pretty sure people can't just wander back and forth in time. What if you met your parents and convinced them not to marry? Then you wouldn't be born. And if that's the case, how could you go back and convince them not to marry? You see what I mean? Just thinking about it makes my head hurt."

"I didn't really go back in time. It was just, sort of, a dream."

"And I was in it."

Lillian nodded. "You were. You've been a good friend to me all along."

"And you returned that favor by telling the possum witch I ate her husband?"

"Of course not. She already knew."

"How could she know?"

"She's a witch," she said.

He gave a slow nod. "That, at least, makes sense—so much as anything can on a night like this."

They crossed the stream, hopping from one stone to another. Lillian managed not to slip this time. She paused on the last rock to dip one paw after another into the water to rinse off the mud.

"What will you do now?" T.H. asked.

"Go back to the farm. What else can I do?"

"But you said that your aunt doesn't recognize you."

"I know. But at least she's alive. And I'll still try to find a way to become a girl again."

"Well, barnyards and foxes don't mix well," T.H. said. "People get the wrong impression when we come by for a visit."

"Like how you might get into the chicken coop?"

He shrugged. "Everyone gets a little peckish."

"Then it's probably a good idea that you don't come. Aunt wouldn't like it, and I don't think the chickens would, either." She paused a moment, then added, "Does that mean I won't see you again?"

"Come into the woods and call for me. If I'm near enough to hear you, I'll come."

"I'll bring you a snack," Lillian told him.

"You don't have to, though I wouldn't say no."

Lillian laughed. "Thanks for being my friend, T.H. I think your mama named you well."

The fox slipped away, a chuckle lingering in the air behind him.

Lillian lifted a paw and studied it in the moonlight. She'd liked having fingers again, but being a kitten was a small price to pay to make things right.

CHAPTER TWENTY-ONE

Lost

illian came upon Aunt still out in the fields with a lantern, calling her name. She ran through the long grass, calling out, but her cries were only meows. The lantern paused on its journey through the meadow. Aunt turned in her direction.

"Oh, kitten," she said, "I only wish my Lillian were as easy to find as you. Where *is* that girl?"

"I'm here, I'm here! Right in front of you."

Aunt bent down and gave her a pat. "I'm so worried about her. She's a good girl. The only thing that would keep her away from home is if something bad

has happened to her. Oh, I'm at my wit's end. She could be lying out there in the woods somewhere with a broken leg, and how would we find her?"

"Don't feel bad. I'm not lost. I'm right here."

But of course Aunt couldn't understand her meowing. She should have asked the possum witch if she had a magic potion like the one she'd stolen from Mother Manan, except this potion would let animals talk to humans. She so wanted to tell Aunt that she didn't have to worry.

Aunt straightened up and peered into the darkness.

"Lillian!" she cried, her voice breaking. "Can you hear me?"

Lillian didn't bother responding. She just followed in Aunt's wake as Aunt slowly made her way down the hill. When Aunt reached the creek, she took the path to the Welches' farm, and Lillian trotted along behind her. The hounds began to bark as they approached the farm a while later, and Lillian gave a nervous cry. She remembered the warning Jack Crow had given her what seemed like ages ago. The dogs might be her friends when she was a girl, but when she was a kitten they'd just see her as a snack.

Aunt scooped Lillian up and continued toward the farmhouse with the dogs sniffing curiously around her. The kitchen door opened before she could reach the back porch, and Earl stood silhouetted by the light behind him.

"Fran?" he said. "What have you got there?"

"It's just a kitten. I'm looking for Lillian. Have you seen her today?"

He shook his head. "It's late for her to be out."

"Don't I know it. Something's happened to her. I can feel it in my bones."

"Let me get a coat," he said, "and we'll help you look. Harlene," he called back into the house, "we've got us a situation here."

~

But even with the three of them scouring the woods, they couldn't find Lillian, because she wasn't lost. They tramped through the woods, their lanterns bobbing in the dark. They called her name, stopping to listen for the faintest response. Finally Harlene and Earl joined Aunt under a large beech tree.

"First thing at dawn," Earl said, "I'll take the wagon into town and we'll get a search party up here."

Aunt nodded. "Thank you. I think I'll just keep looking awhile longer."

Harlene put her hand on Aunt's arm. "What you need to do is get some rest so that you can help in the search tomorrow."

"Maybe you could talk to those Creek boys in the morning," Earl added.

"Good thinking," Aunt said. "They know these woods, and they all like Lillian. They'll help."

"'Course they will," Earl said, "but I was thinking they might be able to track her. Those boys read sign like Preacher Bartholomew can read his Bible."

"But meantime," Harlene said, "you should get some rest."

"I don't know that I could sleep," Aunt said.

"I'll go back with you," Harlene told her. "Maybe she's at the house right now, wondering where you've got to."

"We can hope," Aunt said.

Earl left them to head for home while the two women continued up the long meadows to the farm. Lillian followed behind Aunt and Harlene, wishing she knew some way she could put an end to all this fuss. She felt terribly bad for what Aunt was going through, but at least Aunt was alive. That was a big improvement so far as Lillian was concerned.

But then she remembered how she'd felt when Aunt had died. She stopped where she stood, looking at the two women continuing on into the darkness with their lanterns. She didn't want Aunt to have to go through that. But how was she supposed to fix it?

"I want to be a girl again," she said into the darkness.

CHAPTER TWENTY-TWO

The Apple Tree Man

here was one place where Lillian had always felt safe and content. Up the meadow she went until she got to the apple orchard and the Apple Tree Man's tree. There she lay down under its twisty branches, where she'd happily dreamed so many times before.

She was going to be a cat forever and ever, she realized. And Aunt was going to be awfully sad, and though this wasn't as bad a world as the one that Old Mother Possum had let her experience, she still pined for her life as a girl. What, oh whatever was she going to do?

She wanted to be brave, but she couldn't stop the little mewing sounds that started to come from her throat.

"What's the matter, little kitten?"

Lillian looked up into the boughs of the apple tree, but there was no one up there. Instead, the voice had come from the other side of the tree, where she could make out the shape of a man sitting there on the slope, hidden in the shadows. A man who could understand her.

"I'm not a cat. I'm a girl," she said.

"I know you," the man said, peering closely at her. "You're Lillian. Every morning you bring me my breakfast."

Lillian stood up and peered closer at the man.

"Who are you?" she asked.

"You call me the Apple Tree Man."

Now here is some real magic, Lillian thought, forgetting her troubles for a moment.

A man who lives in a tree. Perhaps he would have some advice for her.

"Can you help me?" she asked.

"That depends on what needs doing, I guess."

For what felt like the thousandth time, Lillian told her story.

"I think maybe I can help you," he said. "I have a madstone in some old corner of my tree. Let me have a look."

Lillian watched as the shadowy figure stood up and stepped into the tree. One moment he was there, just as gnarly and twisty as she'd imagined he'd be, and the next he was gone. She should have been amazed, but seeing as how she'd just done the same at the possum witch's tree, it didn't seem so surprising anymore.

"Here you go," he said, stepping out of the tree again. "You'll need cat magic as well, though."

He offered her a small, smooth, flat stone that was as white as moonlight. When Lillian tried to take it from him, it slid right out of her mouth.

"Let me carry it for you," he offered.

"But carry it where?" Lillian asked.

"I know where," he told her.

He put the madstone in his pocket, picked her up, and set off into the woods. The dark forest, changed by the shadows and moonlight, felt strange and unfamiliar. And then there was a smell in the air— a smell Lillian remembered from when she'd been in the beech tree's clearing. It was the smell of cats, mysterious and wild, and the smell of something else, wilder and older and more secret still.

She was glad to have the Apple Tree Man's company as they approached the beech. It made her feel brave and strong. He set her down and she trotted along beside him now, still marveling that there really was a man living in the oldest tree of the orchard.

But once they got to the beech tree, her confidence faltered.

"What should I do?" she asked.

"Call the cats," he told her.

So she did. She cleared her little cat's throat. "Hello hello," she called. "Please don't be angry, cats, but I need your help again."

But it wasn't the cats that came in response to her call.

A branch creaked in the boughs above, and she thought she heard a rumbling from under the hill, as though old tree roots were shifting against stone. She gave the Apple Tree Man a worried glance, but he wasn't looking at her. His attention was on the other side of the tree.

Lillian gasped when she saw what he was looking at. A huge black panther moved like a ghost in the shadows. She thought her heart would stop in its little cat chest.

"Who . . . ?" she began, but she already knew.

"Lillian," the Apple Tree Man said, "meet the Father of Cats."

"Hello, cousin," the panther said to him. His dark gaze turned to her. "Child, you have upset the balance in this world."

His voice was like the low growl of a grumpy bear woken from its sleep. When he lay down to look at her, he was still much taller than she was, his tail going *pat-pat-pat* on the ground behind him, the way a cat's will before it pounces.

Lillian felt like her heart was going to jump right out of her chest, it was beating so hard. But she had to be brave. She had to try to make things right.

"Please, sir. I'm sorry for the trouble I've caused," Lillian said. "I've learned to be more careful . . . about snakes and consequences and everything. I know things aren't right. I just want to be a girl again. And Aunt needs me, she does."

He cocked his head. "And what is it that you so dislike about the shape of a cat?"

"Oh, nothing. Honestly, I love cats. But I'm really a girl, you see."

"What will you give me if I help you?"

Lillian gulped. She should have seen this coming. Once again, she had nothing to offer. This panther was probably the devil in disguise, and what he really wanted was her soul.

Lillian looked to the Apple Tree Man for help, but

he shook his head as if to say, This you must deal with on your own.

She turned back to the panther. "I don't think I have anything you would want," she said.

"What if I asked you to come away with me for a year and a day?"

Where to? Lillian thought. Down below?

"I—I don't think I could go," she told him. "I'd miss Aunt too much. And she'd be so sad. Have you heard her calling for me down by the creek?"

They were too far away now, but Lillian could almost imagine she could still hear Aunt's voice, calling into the night.

"Mmm," the panther said. Then he, too, looked at the Apple Tree Man. "I've warned my children not to work this magic again, but they didn't listen. You see what problems it causes? A strong lesson is in order, one they will not forget."

"She would have died otherwise."

"Mmm. But there is a price to pay." His tail swished ominously in the grass.

"She means no harm," the Apple Tree Man added, "and has done only good. She always spares grain for the sparrows. She gives your children milk. She brings me a share of her breakfast every morning."

"Mmm," the panther said a third time.

It was a deep, rumbly sound. The sound of him thinking, Lillian realized.

"You've a madstone soaked in milk?" the panther finally asked. "For if I change her, she will need it."

"I have the stone," the Apple Tree Man said. "I can soak it in milk."

"Then do so."

The Apple Tree Man gave her a reassuring smile, then turned and left them, a strange moving figure with his gnarly, twisted limbs.

The whole of the night seemed to be holding its breath as they waited for the Apple Tree Man to return. Lillian listened to the *pat-pat-pat* of the panther's tail tapping the ground and fretted about what kind of payment the Father of Cats would demand of her.

When the panther finally broke the silence, it was not what Lillian expected to hear.

"They say one good turn deserves another," he murmured.

"Please, sir," Lillian said. "That's not why I shared our food and milk."

"I know. And that's why I will help you. But you will still owe me a favor. I might ask it of you. I might ask it of your children, or your children's children. Will you accept the debt?"

Lillian had to gather her courage before she could answer.

"Only—only if no one will be hurt by it," she said.

The panther gave her a grave nod. "That's a good answer," he said. "Now here comes our apple tree friend. Lie down and we will see how we may help you."

Lillian did as she was told. The last thing she saw before she closed her eyes was the Apple Tree Man carrying a tin mug and the deep golden glow that

started up in the Father of Cats' yellow eyes. The last thing she heard was the faint echo of Aunt's voice in the distance, sounding in her imagination, and the low rumbling music of the panther's song as he called up his magic right beside her. Then there was a flare of pain such as she'd felt only once before, when the snake bit her. It lasted just a moment, but it felt like forever before the cool, milk-wet stone was laid against the bite and she drifted away.

CHAPTER TWENTY-THREE

Fairies

Whither she woke again, she and the Apple Tree Man were alone under the beech tree. But she was a girl once more. She sat up, hugging herself, and grinned at him.

"I'm me again," she said.

He smiled. "You were always you. Now you just look more familiar, that's all." He hesitated, then added, "The Father of Cats said he had one word for you, and it was *remember*. Do you understand what he meant?"

Lillian nodded. "It's the payment I owe him. I

have to always carry a debt, never knowing when he might ask for it to be paid. And he said if I don't pay it, then the debt will carry on to my children, or my children's children."

"Does that trouble you?"

Lillian thought about it.

"I don't think so. I made him promise that I'd only help if no one was to be hurt by my help."

The Apple Tree Man smiled. "That was wise of you."

"Do you think he's the devil?" Lillian asked.

That made her companion laugh. "Hardly. The Father of Cats was here before there was such a word as *devil*."

She looked at his wrinkly face and his gnarly limbs.

"Are you a fairy man?" she had to ask. She remembered him stepping into the tree and then back out again with the white madstone in his twisty fingers. But the whole rest of the night had begun to take on the quality of a story she'd been told when she was only half-awake, and it was hard to remember now.

He shook his head. "I'm only what you see: the spirit of an old tree." He looked up into the branches of the beech and laid his hand upon its bark. "Though not so old as this grandfather."

"Do you think the cats will get into trouble?" she asked.

"I hope not. Perhaps your bargain will cover it. It was a good thing they did."

Lillian smiled. "Well, I sure think so."

The Apple Tree Man stood up and took her hand. "Come," he said. "We should go."

"I would like to see the fairies sometime," Lillian said after they'd been walking for a few minutes, already beginning to forget all the wonders she'd seen and experienced.

Everything seemed odd and a little hazy, even this

walk back from the beech tree. She didn't remember crossing the creek, but suddenly here they were, in familiar fields with the orchard nearby.

The Apple Tree Man laughed. "You have only to open your eyes," he said.

"But I do. I run here and there and everywhere with my eyes wide open, but I never see anything. Fairy-like, I mean."

He sat down on the grass and she sat beside him.

"Try looking from the corner of your eye," he said. He lifted a hand and pointed down the hill. "What do you see there?"

She saw the bobbing of Aunt's lantern as she returned from her fruitless search. She saw dark fields, dotted with apple trees and beehives. She didn't see even one fairy.

"Give it a sidelong glance," the Apple Tree Man told her.

So she turned her head and looked at the bob of Aunt's lantern from the corner of her eye.

"I still don't see . . ."

Anything, she was going to say. But it wasn't true. The slope was now filled with small, dancing lights, flickering like fireflies. Only these weren't magical

bugs—they were magical people. Tiny glowing people with dragonfly wings who swooped and spun through the air, leaving behind a trail of laughter and snatches of song.

"Oh, thank you for showing them to me," Lillian said, turning back to her companion.

But the Apple Tree Man was gone.

Lillian reached forward and touched the ground where he'd been sitting. The grass was still pressed flat.

"Good-bye good-bye," she said softly. "Tomorrow I'll bring you a whole plate of biscuits for your breakfast."

Then she jumped to her feet and ran down the slope to where her Aunt walked with slumping shoulders, her gaze on the ground, all unaware of the troops of fairies that filled the air around her.

Acknowledgments

I thank Joe Monti, for wanting more of Lillian's story; Andrea Spooner, for her astute editorial pen; Charles Vess, for bringing to life the pictures in my head; and, of course, my readers, young and not-so-young, who meet me in the pages of my stories and make the solitary art of writing far less lonely. —*Charles de Lint*

First, I want to thank my sister-in-law, June, for telling me her tale of wandering in the woods as a young girl and coming upon a forest glade with its circle of cats. Her story had me running to my studio to put pencil to paper, and the resulting image would eventually inspire this novel. Then, Joe Monti, for asking in the first place, and Andrea, Deirdre, and the whole crew at Little, Brown for many keen insights that helped make my art fit so comfortably with the other Charles's lovely words. And to my wife, Karen, to whom I already owe so much. The art for this book required many, many hours at my drawing board, away from our home, where far too many chores were left undone, but she offered me nothing but encouragement and criticism and delight as each painting was completed. —*Charles Vess*

Artist's Note

Before this story was even written, when it was still just a desire by two old friends to work on a book together, I took Charles de Lint and his wife, MaryAnn, on a hike into the forested hills directly across the street from my home. There we saw an old homestead gradually returning to the earth and the remains of a grove of apple trees. Suddenly we heard a rough voice speaking to us from the branches of a nearby maple. A hunter who had been in his blind since dawn claimed to have seen a large black panther cross the clearing when the early-morning mist still clung to the grass. All was fodder for our tale.

All the paintings in this book were begun using a plain old school pencil, specifically a Miranda Black Warrior 2-HB. I go over the pencil marks with a fine ink outline, using a dip-pen, a Hunts Crowquill 102, and usually a hand-mixed, sepia-toned ink. Then I apply multiple layers of washes of diluted FW colored inks, slowly building up the color. All this is done on Strathmore (4 ply) 500 Bristol paper with a vellum finish, a tough surface that puts up with all my very energetic manipulation of it.

—*Charles Vess*

About This Book

This book was edited by Andrea Spooner and Deirdre Jones and designed by Saho Fujii under the art direction of Dave Caplan and Sasha Illingworth. The production was supervised by Virginia Lawther, and the production editor was JoAnna Kremer. This book was printed on 100gsm Gold Sun Woodfree paper. The text was set in MrsEaves, and the display type is hand-lettered.

CHARLES DE LINT is the much-beloved author of more than seventy adult, young adult, and children's books, including *The Blue Girl*, *Dingo*, *The Painted Boy*, *Under My Skin*, and *A Circle of Cats*, the picture book on which *The Cats of Tanglewood Forest* is based. Well known throughout fantasy and science-fiction circles as one of the trailblazers of the modern fantasy genre, he is the recipient of the World Fantasy, White Pine, Crawford, and Aurora awards. De Lint is a poet, songwriter, performer, and folklorist, and he writes a monthly book-review column for the *Magazine of Fantasy & Science Fiction*. He shares his home in Ottawa, Canada, with his wife, MaryAnn Harris; a cat named Clare; and a little dog named Johnny Cash.

CHARLES VESS is a world-renowned artist and a three-time winner of the World Fantasy Award, among several others. His work has appeared in magazines, comic books, and novels including *The Coyote Road—Trickster Tales*, *Peter Pan*, *The Book of Ballads*, and *Stardust*, written by Neil Gaiman and made into an acclaimed film by Paramount Pictures in 2007. Vess has also illustrated two picture books with Gaiman (*Instructions* and *Blueberry Girl*) that were *New York Times* bestsellers. His art has been featured in several gallery and museum exhibitions across the United States as well as in Spain, Portugal, the United Kingdom, and Italy. He lives on a small farm and works from his studio, Green Man Press, in southwest Virginia.